Jonny Nexus is a London based writer and computer programmer. In his spare time, he writes, reads, watches TV, films and the occasional work of theatre, and engages in twice weekly bouts of extremely bad roleplaying.

Eight years ago, he decided to put his resulting experiences to good use by co-founding the Internet webzine Critical Miss, the self-proclaimed magazine for dysfunctional roleplayers. Since then, Critical Miss has gained several thousand readers along with a reputation that, whilst not being something one could use the phrase "critically acclaimed" in connection with, has made it something of a byword for the less serious side of roleplaying.

Critical Miss has not won any major awards and quite frankly, Jonny wishes that people would stop interpreting his frequent blog rants on the subject as indications that he is in any way bothered.

He is not. Really. Honesty. Especially the whole ENnie nomination thing.

Jonny is now attempting to do to the world of novels what Critical Miss did to the world of webzines, the result being the book that you're currently reading. He probably won't win any awards with this effort either, but if it gets several thousand readers too then he probably won't care.

It should hopefully surprise no-one to learn that "Jonny Nexus" is in fact a pseudonym.

Game Night

By Jonny Nexus

First published in the United States and the United Kingdom
in 2007 by Magnum Opus Press

ISBN 978-1-906402-01-3

10 9 8 7 6 5 4 3 2

www.jonnynexus.com/gamenight/

Magnum Opus Press
29a Abbeville Road
London SW4 9LA

www.magnumopuspress.com

Cover design and art by Jon Hodgson

www.jonhodgson.net

Thanks to Jules, for the love, encouragement
and support that she gave me throughout the
writing of this book;

to James, for the guidance and advice, and for
publishing this book;

to Warren, Bairbre, Stu, Sian and Brian for
the advice, suggestions and feedback, and for
hunting down so many typos;

and to London Underground, for providing
me with my office. Of an eight carriage train
full of several hundred people, I was probably
the only one who was always happy to be
delayed.

"Lord Warrior, a question, if you please? When we solve the riddle, who shall we give the answer to? Who will tell us if we are right, or we are wrong?"

"Ah."

Eridu took a step forward, and began to recite the words he'd waited a lifetime to speak.

"I have many births,
too many to count,
but deaths I have one,
no chance of miscount.
I know where I'm going,
no mistakes I shall make,
but of thoughts and decisions,
I do not partake.
Much movement–"

"Aren't you dead?"

"No!" chant five voices in unison. The figure to the left of the Warrior – the Sleeper, the Lord of Man's Inactivity – blinks in confusion. "But didn't Lord Warrior kill him?"

The AllFather sighs. "Yes. But then he decided that he hadn't actually done it, so we rewound things back to the start."

"Yes, I know. But then he killed him again, didn't he?"

"Yes, and then he decided that he hadn't done that either and we rewound it back again."

"Oh, right."

"Please try to keep up."

Eridu stopped, angry, and glared at the source of the interruption: the rusty armoured warrior with the knackered looking mule.

"Do I look dead?"

"No, sorry. My mistake."

Eridu gave him a final glare, shot a confused glance at the Northland barbarian and got an apologetic shrug in return, and then began once more to recite the words he'd waited a lifetime to speak.

"I have many births,
too many to count,
but deaths I have one,
no chance of miscount.
I know where I'm going,
no mistakes I shall make,
but of thoughts and decisions,

5

I do not partake.
Much movement I have,
yet I seldom alter,
I may twist and turn,
but I'll never falter.
What am I?"

"I hate riddles!" exclaims the Warrior. "The game should be about what our mortals can do, not what we are capable of."

The figure who sits to the Warrior's right nods in reluctant agreement. He is the Dealer, the Lord of Man's Contentment. "Much as it pains me to admit it," he says, "I think Lord Warrior has a point."

"Look, I'm just trying to put a bit of intelligent thought into the game," snaps the AllFather.

"What did the Gatekeeper say again?" asks the Jester. "Something about births and deaths. Did anyone write it down?"

Eridu took a step forward, and began to recite the words he'd waited a lifetime to speak.

"I have many births,
too many to count,
but deaths I have one,
no chance of miscount.
I know where I'm going,
no mistakes I shall make,
but of thoughts and decisions,
I do not partake.
Much movement I have,
yet I seldom alter,
I may twist and turn,
but I'll never falter.
What am I?"

He looked around and saw only five confused and puzzled faces. Perhaps these were not the Visitors.

"What in the bowels of he who rules our basement is that supposed to mean?" snaps the Warrior.

"It's a riddle," smirks the Jester. "It's supposed to be hard."

"Perhaps you should let those with a brain consider it," says the Lady, icily.

"Are you talking to him or me?" asks the Warrior.

"Why would you think I'm only speaking to one of you?"

6

Yann twirled a stalk of wild high grass between his fingers and considered the meaning of the riddle. Many births, but a single death. Moving, yet not moving. Knowing and yet not knowing.

His thoughts swirled, and danced, and coalesced, only to break away to dance again. The Answer was elusive and slippery, like a dying ice salmon swimming for home. It's there, you can feel it; but when you try to grasp it you find only its trail.

He focussed on nothingness, as his Shaman-Father had taught him, turning inward, letting go of the world around him, feeling his thoughts merging as one.

And then the screaming began.

"I sometimes think you belong downstairs," shouts the Dealer.

"No need to get personal," says the Warrior.

"Hard not to," suggests the Jester. The Lady nods in agreement.

"The Gatekeepers have kept this secret for more than twelve thousand of their years," says the Dealer slowly, fighting for calm. "Do you really think you could get hold of it by just slapping the latest incumbent around for a bit?"

"It was worth a try," says the Warrior with a shrug.

Silence descends around the table.

"The Riddle?" suggests the AllFather, finally breaking the silence, only for it to resume, resiliently, after he has finished speaking.

The silence continues, accompanied, but not interrupted, by the occasional questioning glance.

Beneath the table the Dog, the Lord of Man's Loyalty, stirs, half-heartedly licks his balls, and then settles back down to sleep.

Eventually, the Warrior ventures to speak. "I was only joking when I said I was hitting him."

"Right."

"I didn't actually hit him."

"Of course."

The sun fell to the horizon, flared briefly, and then departed, taking day with it and leaving only night. Through it all, Yann let the words of the riddle flow over him, trying to ignore the hunched figure of the Gatekeeper huddling terrified beside the Gate, or the noise of Hill's riding dog Shovel apparently attempting to dig its way under the wall.

"I swear that dog's got some terrier in it," remarked Draag to no-one in particular.

The night continued.

"Can you give us a clue?" asks the Jester, a hopeful smile upon his face.

"What's the point of setting you an intellectual problem if I then just tell you the answer?" replies a depressed AllFather.

The Lady lays a hand upon the AllFather's arm. "No-one's asking you to tell us the answer," she says.

"Just to give us a little clue," adds the Jester.

The AllFather sighs. "Well what's got many starting points and only one end point?"

"Dunno. And what's all that stuff about knowing where to go mean?"

"Well it knows where to go, because its path, its course, is predictable."

"Right. How?"

The AllFather looks around the table. "Anyone?" he asks, a tone of slight desperation in his voice. He gets no response, and continues, haltingly. "See although it twists and turns when looked at from above, when looked at from the side, it's always going in the same direction."

"Which is?" asks the Jester.

"Downwards."

"Downwards?"

"Oh for pity's sake, yes downward! It always flows downward!"

"It flows downward," muses the Lady. "What? Like a river?"

"Yes," mutters a defeated AllFather.

"That would make sense," concedes the Jester. "So the answer's a river, right?"

"Yes" says the AllFather, his head in his hands.

The Jester thinks for a moment. "What about deltas?"

"What about them?" asks the AllFather warily.

"Well in a delta a river splits into many channels, each of which makes its own way to the sea. That would make many deaths. So the answer to the riddle can't be a river because we're looking for something that has a single death."

"The answer," hisses the AllFather through gritted teeth, "is a river, okay?"

It is the Warrior who eventually breaks the resulting silence. "Shall we just give the answer to the Gatekeeper then, and get this farce over with?"

"I'm not sure he's in any real state to receive the answer," says the Dealer, with a hint of bitter sarcasm.

The Lady touches the AllFather on the arm again, and smiles. "Perhaps we should just start over from the top?"

Eridu took a step forward, and began to recite the words he'd waited a lifetime to speak.

"I have many births, too many–"

"River," said the black-clad knight, interrupting.

Eridu fell to his knees, stunned. "You know the answer without hearing the question!" he sobbed. "Truly, you are the Visitors!"

"Yeah, yeah, whatever. You've got the answer, now just open the sodding door."

Eridu stood, and walked on shaking legs to the Gate. He raised his hands to the skies, spoke the sacred words that invoked the power of the Gods, and laid his fingers upon the smooth unmarked metal of the door.

Somewhere inside the mighty structure a thing that was designed to click, clicked, and the door swung smoothly open to reveal the fabled Far Lands that lay beyond the Wall.

Eridu had dreamed of this moment, but had never dared hope for it. He gazed at the view, seconds slowing as though stretched to minutes as he tried to absorb its magnificent beauty, scarcely aware of the Visitors walking past him. A grasp of the arm from the Northlander. Nods from the woman and the halfling. Blank incomprehension from the rusty-armoured fighter. And a mocking sneer from the black-clad knight who'd known the Riddle's answer.

None of it mattered. He'd done his duty. He, the five hundred and seventh Gatekeeper had completed the task so dutifully passed on by the five hundred and six that came before him. Of them all, he alone would enjoy the privilege of a retirement lived with the knowledge that the job was done.

He had just one more task to perform.

"The Gate has opened for you," he said. "And you have passed."

The black-clad knight, hearing his words, turned back to face Eridu. "Oh sorry, yes, almost forgot," he said.

The last thing Eridu ever felt was the sword slicing through his chest and into his heart.

Chapter Two

Tallenna sat back against the tree's cool bark and studied the text before her. To one not versed in the ways of magic, the pages of her spellbook would have gone beyond the merely incomprehensible into realms both chaotic and disturbing. Texts of three different languages fought for space on the smooth vellum, each built upon a different alphabet, and one running left-to-right, one running right-to-left, and one running top-to-bottom. Symbols too crowded into the sprawling mass, spidery traces that spoke of power unleashed.

To an outsider her book was an object to be feared and perhaps mistrusted. But to Tallenna it spoke of home, of the Institute that for more than two thousand years had sat watching the River meet the Western Ocean. The words of the book flowed into her mind, spells as yet uncast settling into their long-worn places, soothing, calming, the reassurance of the known banishing the stresses of the day.

And there had been stresses.

After leaving the Gate the path had forked, and then forked again, and then forked again twice more, and at each fork they had argued – until after three lefts and a bitterly chosen right they'd found themselves lost in the forested canyons that lay beneath the ridge upon which the Wall sat.

The Sun had nearly set by time they'd found a suitable clearing in which to spend the night. While Tallenna took first watch and the chance it offered to memorise the morrow's spells, Yann put up his hide yurt, Hill erected his one man tent, Draag activated the trans-dimensional coffin he claimed to have liberated from a lich's tomb, and Stone simply dropped to the ground.

They slept now, quiet, save for Shovel's snores and occasional snuffles.

Finally, the spells were home once more in Tallenna's mind, and she judged it time for second watch. She nudged Stone awake and whispered, "Your watch."

The fighter nodded and sat up.

Tallenna slept, and the spells slept with her.

The folk reckoned Takes to be the bravest and quickest of them all; for had they not named him "Quick Fingers Shiny Takes" in honour of his prowess?

Some were jealous, true, but even they recognised that he, alone among the folk, had the skill and courage to face the big people who'd spent the afternoon blundering through the canyons.

He edged closer to their camp, carefully pushing fronds aside until at last he could see them. They slept not in the trees, as the folk did, nor in nests of

have set the bushes in front of him on fire. You see him running away down the path."

"Then I'll fire again."

The knuckle-bones bounce and skid across the table, and finally come to a halt; a halt which the Warrior's scowl reveals is not to his liking.

The Jester leans forward, the smirk resumed on his face. "None, none, none, none, none and, yes, that would be another none. I make that none in total?"

"You set some more of the bushes to the side of the path on fire," says the AllFather.

"I'm going to get up if I can, and stagger after him," says the Jester. "Before he sets the whole damned forest on fire."

The AllFather nods, and then speaks. "The monkey scampers away across a fallen log set across the river and disappears into the bushes on the far bank."

The Warrior sits back, hands spread, exaggerated confusion upon his face. "How can the path have crossed the river when it was leading away from the river?"

"It curved round."

"You didn't say that!"

"Well I didn't say it was going in a straight line either. If I stopped to describe every twist and turn of every path or route the game would take forever!"

The AllFather looks at the hourglass that sits atop a pillar at the side of the room, eternal sands endlessly falling through its narrow chamber.

"Somewhere to go?" asks the Jester.

"No, it's just that I was rather hoping to get this whole story arc wrapped up this session."

"Why?" asks the Dealer.

The AllFather pauses for a moment, troubled, unsure of whether to talk, and uncertain of what to say. "Well I'm heading off to this aeon's Conference of Pan-Multiversal Supreme Beings, and it would just be nice to be able to tell the others all about it."

"Well you don't have to have everything finished to tell them about it," the Lady points out.

"No, but you know what they're like." The AllFather looks down, embarrassed. "Especially that cocky one with his oh-so-logical mortal realm."

"The one with the good-looking son?" asks the Lady.

"That's the one. I ask you, what's so impressive about round worlds and–" the AllFather makes quote marks with his fingers, "-celestial mechanics."

"Internal consistency?" suggests the Jester.

"Making belief in a supreme creator a matter of faith rather than fact?" adds the Dealer.

The AllFather glares at the two of them in turn. "Well that's as maybe, but does he have to be so smug about it? I swear, if he tells me once more about how he created his entire realm in six days, I'll..."

He breaks off. "Anyway, back at the camp–"

The Warrior breaks in. "Camp? I was heading off across the log after the monkey!"

"But the monkey's long gone!"

"How? I was right behind it! It's not my fault you chose to pause the game to spend five minutes whining about how other people have better realms than you."

The AllFather sighs. "Fine, you're right behind the monkey. But the log is quite narrow, and very slippery, and it really is a raging torrent underneath it.

"Whatever. I'm walking onto the log."

"You'll need two successes to make it across."

The knuckle-bones dance across the table and into an extended period of silence. Five faces look at the AllFather waiting for judgement.

"Okay. One success. Well you make it a little way onto the log, but are then halted by a particularly slippery spot. You think you should be able to retrace your steps."

"I'll continue!" declares the Warrior, casting the knuckle-bones once more. "Cursed bloody things!" he shouts when he sees the result. He picks the knuckle-bones up and throws them down in front of the Sleeper, dragging the Sleeper's knuckle-bones over to him as replacements.

"Getting superstitious, are we?" asks the Jester in a cheery tone.

The AllFather looks pained. "You're wobbling very badly and need to regain your balance. You need one success."

"Fine!" snaps the Warrior. The knuckle-bones bounce angrily across the table, but when they rest it is clear from his scowl and the Jester's smirk that the result is not what he hoped.

"So I suppose I'm in the river now, am I?" shouts the Warrior.

"No," replies the AllFather, "you've slipped off the log but one success will mean that you've managed to grab hold of it as you fall past."

The Warrior scoops up the knuckle-bones and again throws them across the table.

The Jester leans in to count the result. "Now you're in the river!" he declares.

Still clutching his halfling-hood, Hill reached the end of the path just in time to see Draag first wobble one way, then the other, slip, make a desperate attempt to catch the log as he fell past it, miss, and finally plunge into the river, the splash of his entry nearly swallowed by the raging torrent's foamy spray.

He rose, sank, rose again – right hand still defiantly clutching his night-black sword – and then sank a final time.

Shovel trotted up and looked at his master.

Hill stared at the foaming waters for a moment, shrugged, and then whistled at the dog. "Come on boy, let's get back."

Chapter Three

Today was a day of tragedy and grief, a day to wail at the winds that rode the mountains and a day to rage at death.

For all the years that Pannon had lived and for many years before, his great-uncle Eridu had sat at the Gate. Others had ridiculed, laughed, jeered, and even ostracised him; but not Pannon. He knew not what it was his great-uncle was doing, nor why; but he knew it was being done both well and worthily.

At the start of every day of Pannon's life, his great-uncle had left the village and ascended to the Gate, returning only when the Sun dipped below the horizon.

Until today. This morning Eridu had left, cheerful as always, and hale too, though showing perhaps the age that weighed upon him. But as night fell he did not return. It was Eridu's niece Rheanan, Pannon's mother, who had noticed the absence of a light at his window and who, checking, had found his home empty and his coat still gone. It was she who had dispatched Pannon on the search. And it was the search that had taken Pannon to the Gate, where he'd found his great-uncle's body, fallen such that his face was tilted to the Gate he'd guarded, lifeless eyes set as though they were looking beyond its metal surface to the Far Lands that were said to lay beyond.

Now Pannon returned, picking his way down the bank of the river that sprouted from the ground before the Wall, his great-uncle's body cradled in his arms. His grief was near absolute, but the way was dark and treacherous, and so alertness was forced upon him where a daze would better sit.

A movement in the river caught his eye; a thrashing perhaps; a struggle even. He carefully laid the body of his great-uncle upon the ground and approached the water's edge.

It was the eyes that Yann first noticed, observing the camp through a gap in the surrounding foliage. They were brown, a deep brown, with large focussed pupils. They spoke of thought. They spoke of intelligence. They moved, and searched, weaving a pattern that could only indicate a desire for understanding , or possibly – as even Yann would later be forced to admit – a search for things worth taking.

He moved slowly across to the reading Tallenna, ignoring Hill, who, having now reached the tricky central pole stage of tent erection, was somewhere in the interior of a pile of softly cursing canvas.

Tallenna looked up at his approach, saw his indicative glance, looked in that direction, and nodded.

Dealer means. He is pointing out that our mortals do not know that Draag has survived, nor that he waits at the Gate, and so have no reason to return to the Gate to open it."

"Oh, I see," says the Sleeper, nodding in a manner whose hesitancy clearly indicates that he does not.

The Warrior shoots an angry glare at the Dealer. "This is about the Gatekeeper isn't it? You were angry that I killed him, and now you're trying to manipulate your way to a situation where I am disadvantaged as a result!"

"There is no manipulation required, Lord Warrior. You did kill him, and now you are disadvantaged as a result."

There is an angry stare-off that is finally broken by the Jester.

"Can we get back to the monkey situation?"

Many years ago, Yann's shaman-father had inducted him into the mysteries of the inner voice, that part of the soul that lives through its many incarnations, that part of the soul that holds the wisdom thus gained.

An inner voice spoke to him now, but it was not his, for while his inner voice was calm and soothing, the voice that spoke now was urgent and jarring. It sought not to suggest but to demand, and not to aid but to exploit.

Yann wanted to stay. Wanted to rest until morning, then resume their trek down the valley. But the voice would not let him. It nagged, pleaded, demanded, and whined.

Finally, he stood.

"We need to go back to the Gate."

Another silence settles upon the table, broken only by the soft whooshing of the sands though the hourglass that stands at the side of the room, and the rhythmic licking that emanates from beneath the table.

The AllFather takes a few moments to stroke the Dog, then returns his attention to those sitting before him. "So what would you have your mortals do?"

Silence.

"Would it help if I gave you the description again?"

The Lady gives him a resigned smile. "It has been a little while."

"Fine." He clears his throat, and begins to read from his notes. "You have been reunited at the Gate, after Yann... intuitively realised that you needed to return there."

The AllFather attempts to catch the Dealer's eye, but the Dealer is still staring hard at the stretch of table he's been staring at since the argument ended in his defeat.

"You now stand once again before the fabled Far Lands, a realm of such enchanted beauty that your senses are momentarily overwhelmed. A path leads down the slope for several hundred feet before branching, one branch descending into the forests, one branch climbing along the side of the ridge."

He looks up.

"Well?"

He receives only silence. "Which way do you want to go?"

"Well which way do we need to go?" asks the Jester.

"Look! We've had this argument once this session already. If I set you an intellectual challenge, then the challenge is for you to solve it. It's up to you to discover the path to your destination."

"So it's a destination then?"

"Well, yes," the AllFather answers uneasily. "But I'm not playing a game of questions here. Stop fishing."

"Who's fishing?"

"You are."

"What, in asking if our destination's a destination? What possible information did I get by asking that?"

"None."

"Exactly."

"Right."

Sand falls. The Jester examines his nails, leaving the Dealer and the Warrior to their sulky glares, the Lady to her thoughts, and the Sleeper to his daydreaming.

The sand continues to fall.

"Well just pick a way!"

Chapter Four

For as long as men had stood before the Wall, which was as long as men could remember, they had spoken of what might lie beyond.

They had talked about the Far Lands, but that was a merely a name and not a description, for the truth was that talk as they might, and speculate as they did, the Wall was a barrier beyond which none could see.

This complete absence of knowledge was something that was becoming very apparent to Tallenna as she studied her almanac, a magical tome whose speck-small etchings claimed to contain the sum of all human knowledge.

There was indeed much there about the Far Lands. But most of that was myth and legend – and most of what wasn't myth and legend concerned the Prophecy that had led them to the Gate. And as she already knew, the Prophecy was remarkably short of detail as to precisely why they should go to the Gate.

She heard a shout from Yann, and looked up. It appeared they were moving again.

She sighed, and closed the book.

The people of Yann's Northlands home measured time according to the progress of the Sun, with each day progressing from Sun-Here through Sun-There before ending at Sun-Gone. In the years he'd spent travelling with his current comrades however, he'd learned to judge the day's progress according to a different scale; from optimism through bickering to the inevitable screaming row.

This day had started early with the night-time walk from the forest clearing to the Gate, and having started early the day worked hard to keep ahead of schedule, with the first verbal snappings starting over the breakfast of pan fried beans, and the first full-scale row breaking out a little after Hill's mid-morning snack-break.

The group followed a flexible rota when it came to rows. Sometimes the row would be between Draag and Yann. Sometimes it would be between Draag and Tallenna. Many times it would be between Draag and Hill. On some rare occasions it would be a team event, with a combination of Yann, Hill and Tallenna duelling it out with Draag.

At this point – at around what Yann judged as Sun-Nearly-There but which Tallenna had just announced was two minutes past eleven – it was Draag and Hill who had assumed the set roles of arguers.

"Look it's this way. It's obviously this way. If you can't see that it's this way it's because you're either too short to see it or too stupid to understand what you're seeing or both."

"Bollocks!"

Draag looked pointedly to the right, his horse Skull blowing air from its non-existent lungs through its non-existent nostrils and pawing the ground with its front skeletal leg.

This display was totally lost on Hill, for the very good reason that he was currently looking, just as determinedly, left, his mount Shovel excitedly scratching at the ground with an animated rear leg.

Tallenna chose that moment to point forward, midway between where the two protagonists were choosing to orient themselves, and point out something they appeared somehow to have missed.

"Isn't that a house over there?"

The house was a small house, not particularly distinguished in appearance, and nestled discretely into a forest clearing in a manner that could be interpreted as being either in harmony with nature or a hasty last-minute insertion into reality. Certainly, it did not evoke images of the legendary Far Lands, being as it was of simple timber construction with a homely tiled roof.

"Looks like a dump," declared Draag.

"Total," added Hill in a rare piece of agreement. He fed a small piece of honey dried banana chip to the monkey, ignoring the suspicious look that Draag shot him. "But then again, where there's houses there's usually people, and where there's people, there's people you can ask things."

Tallenna smiled at him. "I would have thought you'd have said that where there are people, there are possessions you can steal?"

"You just do the talking love, and let me worry about what needs stealing. Anyway, are we going to head on down and have a chat or just sit here watching it for the rest of the day to see if it moves?"

Around forty minutes of detailed strategy discussion and five minutes of action later, Hill combat-rolled onto the house's veranda and found himself face to face with a kindly old man.

"Would you like some tea?" the old man asked.

The old man sat them down at a polished wooden table, upon which sat bone china saucers cradling bone china cups, and poured strong dark tea from a bone china tea-pot.

"Many years I have been here," said the old man when he'd finished pouring, "And few I have known. You are the first to come here for several years."

"Yeah, yeah whatever," muttered Draag. "All aboard the clue-coach and off

24

we go."

"Who else has come here to speak to you?" asked Tallenna.

The old man held up a hand. "I must warn you, here, now. I am he who answers. That is my role in life. But answer all questions I cannot. Three questions only can I answer, three questions for all five of you, three questions for all of your lives. So it is decreed. Think both wisely and carefully, for however many questions you may ask me, I shall answer only the first three."

"Why?" asked Stone.

"Because it is decreed. You now have two questions left."

"That was a bit mean, wasn't it?" says the Jester.

"Yes it was," replied the old man. "And you now have only one question left."

A controlled uproar breaks out at the table as four gods attempt to make their displeasure felt in sentences and statements that, while passionate, cannot under any circumstances be interpreted as a question.

"That wasn't a question!" shouts the Jester.

"Yes it was," replies the AllFather.

"But it wasn't a question to him," shouts the Warrior. "It was a question to you!"

"Exactly!" shouts the Dealer.

"I think they've got a point," says the Lady.

"So how many questions have we got left?" asks the Sleeper.

"None," replied the old man. "Thank you very much. I hope you enjoyed the tea."

"And what exactly was the point of that farce?" asks the Dealer.

"He asking you, by the way," the Jester tells the AllFather sarcastically. "And not the old man. Just in case you were confused."

"There was no point," the AllFather replies. "There was an opportunity you could have used. You chose not to." He reaches down to give the Dog a couple of pats, and gets a few licks of the hand in return. "Which was somewhat ironic given that you spent a considerable amount of time deciding just how to knock on the front door."

"There could have been anything in there!" shouts the Warrior. "How were we supposed to know that it was just an old man?"

The Dealer interrupts him with a waved finger. "You don't think that a combat approach with dual flanking movements and arranged arcs of covering fire was a bit more than was necessary?"

"As I was saying, there could have been any level of threat in there."

"There still might be," the Jester points out. "I think the old man might want us to leave."

"As I said, thank you, and I hope you enjoyed the tea!" The old man reached forward, grasped the saucer whose opposite edge Draag was grasping, and tugged. The cup clattered around the saucer, the tea inside slopping this way and that, with that eventually winning out over this.

"Oy!" shouted Draag. "I haven't bloody finished yet!" He ripped the cup and saucer combination out of the old man's grasp. "In fact, I haven't actually bloody started yet."

He went to take a sip – more out of sheer bloody-mindedness than any real desire for refreshment – then paused, realising that it might contain more than tea.

"Is it any good?" he asked Hill, who was sitting opposite him.

"Dunno," Hill replied. The halfling took a deep slurp, gurgled the liquid around his mouth, swallowed, and then entirely failed to convulse, choke or die. Finally, he stopped lip-smacking and ventured a verdict. "Not bad."

"Good," said Draag, now taking a sip, pointedly ignoring the old man who stood at the head of the table, glowering at him. "I could do with some refreshment. It's been a long day."

"I would be grateful if you would leave my house," the old man shouted to no-one in particular, which turned out to be quite appropriate, because it turned out that no-one was listening. (Strictly speaking, they might have been listening, but if they were, they didn't appear to have any interest in actually obeying).

"Now look," said Tallenna in a friendly tone. "Mister? I'm sorry, I don't know your name?"

The old man sniffed. "I am he who answers. I have no need of a name."

"If you are he who answers," said Hill, "Then not being able to answer the question 'what is your name?' isn't a terribly good start."

"You asked me your questions, and I answered them. Now I am asking you something!"

"And what's that?" asked Stone.

"I'm asking you to get out of my bloody house," screamed the old man.

"Oh, okay," said Stone, standing up, and turning for the door. "Sorry."

"Where the hell are you going?" shouted Draag.

"He wants us to leave," replied Stone, confused.

"Yes, but we're not leaving, are we? Not until he actually answers some proper questions."

"Oh. Okay. So I'll just sit back down, shall I?"

"Yes."

26

The old man drew himself up. "I shall give you one final warning. Get. Out. Of. My. House."

Draag took a slow sip of tea. "No."

"You have spurned my warnings and now you shall face the consequences!" screamed the old man.

"Yeah, yeah, whatever," said Hill. He attempted to replicate Draag's nonchalant sip but was unable to do so due to the near instantaneous exploding of his tea cup and the resultant shower of tea that splattered across the faces of all those sitting at the table.

Draag moved like lightning. Talking was talking, but this was combat, and combat was what he lived for. He launched himself upward, kicking the chair away as he did so and unsheathing DeathSinger from its lead-encased sheath.

The frail old man was gone now; in his place stood a screaming force of nature whose long white hair reached out in grasping tentacles and whose long bony fingers sprayed purple fire across the cluttered room. Dog-like devils erupted from the walls and launched themselves at the intruders.

Draag ducked beneath a jet of purple fire, parried the biting jaws of one devil wolf and then thrust DeathSinger straight through the heart of another.

Across from him he could see Hill dancing, dagger in front of him, Yann weaving, the quarterstaff in his hands whirling faster than the eye could see, and Tallenna crouched against the far wall, hands shaping magic, lips speaking the ancient words that would send it on its way.

"Cover me!" he screamed to a room too small to contain the chaos exploding within it, launching himself at the thing that stood where the old man had once been. Fire bathed across him, burning, stinging, but then repulsed by a soothing field of magic that spread across him, clear but sparkling, repulsing the flame.

Then he was through and upon the thing, cutting, tearing, a savage swing followed by a brutal stab. Time slowed, halted even. Consciousness shrunk to a pinprick. DeathSinger was all; swinging, parrying, killing. Magic swirled around him - the thing's attempts at defence, and Tallenna and Yann's counters - but it was nothing to him. All that mattered was the attack.

Finally, he felt a hand on his shoulder.

Yann.

"He's down. He's out. Leave it."

Where once a house had stood, a house stood no more. Before him, bloodied, dying perhaps, was the crumpled figure of the old man. All around were burned and broken bricks, scattered across the clearing for a score or

27

more yards. Nearer stood the broken remains of table and chairs and bone-china crockery, the standing figures of Tallenna, Yann and Hill, and the still-sitting figure of Stone, who sat in his chair holding a cup and saucer and looking for all the world like a man trying to work out why he was no longer sitting at a table when he had not at any point moved.

Tallenna bent down and examined the old man. "He's alive, but barely." She looked up at Yann. "If I cast a bind upon him, can you heal him?"

He nodded, and added his nature-powered magic to the scholarly words of power she spoke. The old man's eyes flickered open.

"What is it you want of me?"

Draag crouched down in front of him. "We want you to answer some more questions."

The AllFather sighs. "This isn't a situation where violence will achieve your aims. The Answerer is tasked with answering three questions only."

"So he's got a name now, has he?" asks the Jester.

"Pardon?"

"He's got a name?"

"Yes. He's called the Answerer."

"But he said he didn't have a name!"

"Look. It's what I call him. It's not what he calls himself."

"Well we know that. Or he'd have said that it was his name."

"Good. I'm glad we are all in agreement."

The Warrior taps his fingers upon the table's marble surface. "What would have happened if we had arrived in two groups?"

The AllFather frowns. "Well you'd have arrived in two groups. I'm not quite sure I understand what you are saying."

"Would we have had three questions per group?"

"Well, yes. I suppose that is what would have happened. But you didn't arrive in two groups, did you?"

The Warrior sits back in his chair, and looks around at his fellow gods, indicating with a wave that any of them should feel free to join in.

It is the Lady who takes up his offer. "That does seem a bit arbitrary."

"I have to agree," adds the Dealer. "After all, what's his motivation? You are saying that he will defend to the death the principle that he will give us only three answers – and yet if Tallenna and Yann had continued watching from the flanking cover for five more minutes before entering the house he would have given them three further questions."

"Well not if they'd turned up five minutes later!"

"Well how long then?" demands the Warrior. "Ten minutes? An hour? A day? What's the reset period?"

"Reset period? Look, you turned up in one group, so three

questions is all you get, and that's that."

The Dealer breaks the resulting silence. "And I'm also troubled by the way that he tricked us into wasting our questions. It seems malevolent, cruel even."

"It's what he does. It's his role in the world."

"Seems a strange role," the Jester remarks. "So what's the odds of three more questions?"

The old man looked around the wreckage that had once been his home, and at the four, no five, mysterious adventurers who had transformed it so.

"I tested you earlier, and you proved worthy. Now I shall answer three actual questions. But choose wisely, for I will answer three questions only. Please ask me your first question."

Hill held up a hand. "Give us a moment."

"Of course." The old man felt an urgency - for tea he realised. For a moment he considered scrabbling through the wreckage that crunched underfoot in search of any intact fragments of his tea set. But upon reflection he considered that the cause of preserving his dignity necessitated his not engaging in such an attempt. And so he sat, on the one surviving chair, and watched from afar as the five adventurers gathered some way off in a huddle from which only the occasional urgent whisper emerged.

Finally, they approached him, and the female sorceress whose magic had bound him, spoke. "What is it that we should do, now we have come to these lands beyond the Wall?"

The old man considered the question for a moment. "That is not a question, but a request for advice. If you wish me to answer then you must make it more specific."

He watched as they retreated once more to their huddle, returning several minutes later. This time, it was the barbarian shaman who spoke.

"Someone once built the Wall and the Gate and tasked the Gatekeepers with allowing only those who solved the riddle to pass through to these lands. Why did they do this?"

The old man nodded a satisfied nod. "That is a well-asked question, and one worthy of my answer. The Wall and the Gate were built to select a group of skilled and resourceful adventurers."

That answer elicited a round of satisfied, and proud, nods and glances - which then quickly morphed into puzzled frowns as further questions presumably appeared in the minds that controlled those faces. Tight-lipped, they gave him brief nods of thanks before retreating to their huddle.

Several more minutes elapsed, broken only by the arrival of one resourceful and / or cheeky squirrel, who having darted in from a nearby tree began, after a few nervous glances, to root through the wreckage in search of food.

Snatches of conversation drifted across the clearing to the old man. Words like "Why" and "Who" blended in with "Wall" and "Gate".

Finally, the party of adventurers returned once more. This time it was the black-clad knight who spoke. "Why did the people who built the Wall and the Gate need or want to select a group of skilled and resourceful adventurers?"

The old man leaned forward in his chair and paused, not because he didn't know the answer, for he did, but because an answer such as this deserved its moment in history.

"The group is required in order to perform a mission that will save the entire world, a mission that only a team rich in skill and resourcefulness could accomplish."

The group nodded at that, and turned to retreat once more. But then the black-clad knight paused, and turned back.

"Will those who successfully perform this mission receive fame and fortune as a result?"

The old man replied without hesitation. "Undoubtedly."

Chapter Five

The arguments of the morning continued through the afternoon, and each time they flared Draag repeated the same, specific point.

"There is no point finding out how to do the mission until we know if the mission is worth doing!"

Yann would then ask if saving the entire world was not reason enough, Hill would crack one of three jokes that he'd thought up during the first round of arguments, and Tallenna would attempt to guide the conversation back onto the subject of just what to do next.

"Well that's easy!" declared Draag, on the fourteenth argument cycle. "We simply find the people who built the Wall and find out what it is they want us to do!"

"We are not talking about something built in my mother's time, or my mother's mother's time, or even my mother's mother's mother's time," Yann pointed out patiently. "The Wall was built when men were still newborns upon the surface of the world. It is old beyond imagining, a thing from before recorded time."

"Either they are still here, in which case we will find them. Or they are not, in which case we won't. Nothing the old man could have told us would have in any way changed that fact."

"No," said Hill. "We'd just have known where to look."

"The people who built the Wall will be known to someone. They will either be the rulers of this land, or known to those rulers. So our first task must be to find those rulers."

"How do we do that then?" asked Hill.

"We find some of their subjects and ask them who rules them."

"Isn't that the first task then?"

Three days and two nights later, the party emerged from the forest and met for the first time an inhabitant of the Far Lands, semi-sentient monkeys and implausible seers excepted.

Hill, who as usual was leading the way, reined Shovel in. A man leaned against a tree's trunk at the forest's edge, skilfully stripping the bark from a length of yew. He stood taller than both Yann and Draag and moved with an agile grace. Silver-blond hair fell from his head to his shoulders, framing a face whose beauty was almost shocking. His clothes were woven of fine and many coloured thread and were so finely made that they moved with his body as though they were a second skin. The most striking feature though was the pair of sharply pointed ears that poked through his flowing locks.

The man looked down at Hill, smiled, and resumed his task, apparently unconcerned. Hill looked over his shoulder at his following companions, and whispered.

"Looks like we've got an elf."

"It's not an elf!" the AllFather insists.
"Well it looks like an elf."
"It might look like an elf, but it isn't an elf. There are no elves. Has your mortal ever met an elf?"
"Not until now, no."
"He hasn't met one now. That's not an elf!"
"Well what is it then?"
The AllFather sighs, and tries to avoid contemplating the point of it all. "You don't know what he is, because you haven't asked him."

Hill motioned to the others to stay back within the forest, and then rode slowly forward, stopping some way short of the bark-stripping man.

"Hail, fellow! How goes you?"

The man stopped stripping and looked across at Hill. "I am well, small stranger."

He turned his attention back to the length of yew, carefully placing his knife to lift another strip of bark.

"What are you?" barked Hill, trying not to let the remark about his stature get to him.

"What do you mean, what am I?"

Hill indicated himself. "I am a halfling." He pointed down at Shovel. "This is a dog." He pointed a thumb over his shoulder. "My companions behind me are men. What are you?"

The man paused for a moment, and then laughed. "That is a strange question to ask, little fellow, but one I now understand. Why it matters I do not know, but since it apparently does, I can tell you what I am. I am a Weshen, and my people are the Wesh."

"Okay," said Hill. "Thanks."

He wheeled Shovel round and rode back to where the others were waiting. "The elf says he's a Weshen and that his people are the Wesh."

"I say we kidnap him, take him back into the forest, and question him!"

The Dealer shoots a despairing glance at the Warrior. "In the name of all, why?"

"Why not?" the Warrior replies. "He is on his own, against the five of us, and possesses no weapons save a small wood-cutting knife. He sits defenceless before us and yet we waste time debating."

The AllFather clears his throat. "The Weshen appears to have noticed your urgent debating. He has put down his knife and is looking towards you with a quizzical expression on his face."

The Dealer cuts in before the Warrior has a chance to speak. "I will walk over to him and place my staff before him, on the ground. I am Yann, I will tell him, from the lands beyond the Wall. Please, let me speak with you and your people and learn the wisdom of this land."

The Warrior curses under his breath, and then speaks. "You go off like a lamb to the stew pot if you want, but I'm staying here. And don't expect me to come riding in to rescue you when it turns out they're flesh-eaters."

The village was like nothing Hill had ever seen. A cluster of jewelled marble buildings sat on a gentle slope that led down through a flower speckled meadow to a reed flanked river beyond. Impossibly beautiful people glided through the cobbled streets carrying riches that thirty seconds ago had been beyond Hill's dreams.

All his life Hill had been able to smell money, and whoever these elves were, and whatever the hell they called it, money in quantity was what they had.

He wriggled his fingers and cracked a few joints.

Time to get to work.

The village was like nothing Yann had ever seen. He'd had been born beneath the open skies and raised upon the endless plains, his hide yurt leaving no blemish on the landscape and no mark upon the world. He'd seen many buildings built by so-called civilised men. Some were great edifices, built by kings to speak to future generations. Others were pitiful hovels, built by paupers to shelter them from the weather they feared and misunderstood.

But to Yann that mattered not.

He cared only that they scarred the world, tore chunks from its flesh and put hooks into its skin. Of all the constructions the men of cities called buildings, he'd not seen one that was in harmony with the world.

Until now.

The village was like nothing Tallenna had ever seen. She had grown up in the City, spending her childhood playing tag through its teeming back alleys, her adolescence running goods through its under-street catacombs, and her adulthood studying magic at the Institute's gleaming spires.

The people of the City said that it contained everything that existed in the world: every creed and colour of people; every form of goods or device; every craft and skill; and every type of building ever built.

Tallenna had believed so too.

33

But no longer.

Wenna was the oldest Weshen in the community, perhaps the oldest of the Wesh anywhere. Certainly, he knew of none older, having seen his contemporaries grow frail and renew one by one as the millennia had gone by.

All the Wesh in the village understood what the visitors were; knew that they were four Men, one of whom was female, and one halfling; knew what this meant. But for them this was learned knowledge, facts and tales passed down from age to age.

Only Wenna had previously seen men with his own eyes, for only Wenna was old enough to remember the time before the Wall cut across the Land, when men were young and the lands of the Wesh stretched across the whole of the Land, from coast to coast.

Two of the younger ones had been sent to tell him of the coming of the Men. He had been two months into the one hundred and forty-seventh year of a meditative trance when they'd opened his door, stepped through the inch high dust that covered the floor, and gently shaken him awake.

He knew not their names, for they were barely into their second centuries and bore the awed expressions of ones who knew him only as an old man who slept. But they'd stayed with him as he bathed and dressed and then had led him to the village's central meeting place, where three of the Men – including the woman and the halfling – were waiting.

"This must be their leader," declares the Warrior, interrupting the AllFather's description. "Be careful. He will be probing for information, so give nothing away until he starts revealing what we want to know."

The AllFather looks up from his notes. "Your mortal is not there. You know nothing of what is happening."

"Of course," replies the Warrior. He smirks, and looks around the table. "Pretend that was never said."

He settles back in his chair, and waves the AllFather to continue.

It had taken Draag more than three hours to work his way down the slope to the edge of the village, dragging himself on his elbows all the way. Once there, he waited for several minutes, silently observing, safely shielded by the meadow's long grass.

Whatever the village's defences were, they were hidden well enough to evade his searching. The Wesh were clearly adversaries not to be underestimated.

He would stay where he was.

And watch.

The next three days passed Yann in a blur, an intoxicating mix of sights and sounds and ideas and sensations. The Wesh were a noble people. If he'd had a lifetime to spend with them, he would have, and that would still have been a lifetime too few for all that he wanted to learn from them.

But before all was the mission.

"They are being obstructive. It has been three days now and all they have talked of is philosophy. They have refused even to identify their leaders!"

The Dealer took a deep breath. "They have no leaders in the sense we understand it."

"They must have. Ask the old one again. I think he's stalling."

"Look! You're not there!" protests the Dealer.

"Actually, where are you?" adds the Jester.

"I am continuing to covertly observe the village."

"You've been lying in a field for three days?"

"No he hasn't," says the AllFather, breaking in. "He went back to the camp in the forest."

"No I did not. I never said anything of the sort."

The AllFather blinks. "You're saying that your mortal has been lying in a field for three days and two nights?"

"Yes."

"Without moving?"

"He has a paladin's endurance and mental discipline."

"Without eating?"

"He has emergency trail rations."

"Without attending to his physical needs?"

"Physical needs? What are you talking about?"

The AllFather coughs. "He will need to relieve himself."

"You've never worried about that before!" the Warrior shouts. "Not once have you ever asked when my mortal was relieving himself!"

"You've never claimed he was spending three days lying in a field before," protests the AllFather.

"Fine. Draag will relieve himself where he lays. He cares not for his own personal comfort."

"There's the other stuff as well," the Jester adds laughing.

"He cares not for that either!"

"Fine."

"But you're still not there!" says the Dealer.

The halfling-folk of the County had an expression that Hill had lived his life by: greed should always be a servant and never a master.

So on the first night Hill had merely watched and observed.

On the second night he had planned.

And on the third night he had acquired.

Several times.

Now, on the morning of the fourth day, he lay back in the sumptuous quarters the Wesh had provided for him and mentally counted through the possessions that now lay hidden beneath his bed. The finest cutlery, crafted from gold and garnished with gems. Intricate devices whose purposes he could only guess at. Balms and spices and iridescent liquids.

It could only be described as riches beyond calculation, although Hill had decided to try anyway and had come up with a figure in excess of fifty thousand gold crowns.

This land was nearly perfect, save for one thing.

That the beds were too big he could live with.

That the women were too big he could not.

Tallenna had always been a quick learner; it was, after all, her quick mind that had caused the mighty Institute to recruit a rag-clad orphan from the streets and teach her the ways of magic.

In three days and three nights spent at the Wesh village, Tallenna had gained knowledge that might take years to record, were she ever to return to the Institute's library, and its thousands of miles of shelves.

But when the Institute had taught her magic they'd taught her duty also, and her duty now was to the mission the Prophecy had led her to. In all that the Wesh had said – and what they'd said was rich and wide-ranging – there had been nothing that gave either insight or clue about the mission.

She and Yann were sat in the village's central debating hall, where they had spent much of the previous three days. As far as she could tell, the hall served as combination court, temple, school and meeting place. Beside them, Stone sat.

Once more, she tried to elicit information. "Who is in charge of you? Who tells you what to do?"

The old Weshen, Wenna, sighed. "No one tells us what to do."

"So you can do anything you like? You could kill someone if you wanted to?"

"No Weshen would do such a thing."

Yann leaned forward. "But there must be times when people disagree on what should be done?"

"There are such times, yes."

It was at this moment that the doors to the meeting room crashed open, and a highly bedraggled Draag strode in. He let the doors slam shut behind him, and struck a pose that would have been noble were it not for the mud, excrement and dried, broken grass that covered his once gleaming armour.

"I am Draag, Paladin of Darkness." He walked over to the female Weshen who stood behind what Tallenna had, over the last three days, deduced to be an altar.

"A pint of your finest ale, fair maiden!" he boomed, slapping a gold crown down upon the altar's marble surface. He leaned forward, and winked a mud-encrusted eyelid at her. "And take one for yourself!"

Hill was in his room when the trouble started. Having spent most of the night exercising a deep-rooted part of his instinctive racial heritage – that being the urge to collect shiny things – Hill had planned on spending most of the following day sleeping.

It was a good plan, and one that Hill was so determined to follow that not even the angry shouts that penetrated his quarters' stone walls were enough to wake him. They were, alas, enough to wake Shovel though, who through a mixture of barking and snout-prodding proceeded to wake his master up.

Hill immediately realised that he had broken one of the ten cardinal rules of the Thief's Code, number four to be precise.

Stay not at the scene of the crime, for that is where you will most likely be caught.

He quickly scooped the night's haul into a couple of sacks and then stuffed the sacks into his saddle bags, discarding any unnecessary and bulky items (spare underwear, toilet rolls, dog rations) as required to allow the booty to fit.

Not much more than forty-five seconds after the first shout, Hill was riding down what passed for the village's main street, having slapped the saddle onto Shovel, shoved the still-sleeping monkey onto the front of the saddle, and jumped on.

Ahead was the large building that stood in the centre of the village and which looked, to Hill's admittedly unpious eyes, like a church. Hill had stayed clear of the building over the previous days, heeding the lessons contained within rule number seven of the Code.

Steal not from churches or temples, for that will make people really, really angry.

Three screaming Weshen men ran into the church through its open doorway, their silken robes flapping around them. A moment later, they ran back out of the doorway; they were still screaming, but now it was because they were on fire.

Hill pressed in a knee and swerved Shovel into a hard right, away from the church.

"Come on boy," he cooed. "I really, really think we don't want to be here."

The sounds of fighting grew distant behind him.

Chapter Six

Strange and wondrous as the Far Lands were, the sun still rose and the sun still set, and it was just falling below the horizon when Tallenna heard Yann's plains-dog call echoing through the forest.

She paused for a moment and spoke a few words, casting a simple cantrip that reached out for the words and drew a glowing thread through the forest that only she could see.

Carefully she followed the thread, stepping cautiously through a landscape still not fully familiar to one urban-bred such as she, despite the years she'd spent on wilderness quests.

A few minutes later she emerged into a clearing, finding Yann seated upon a fallen oak trunk, preparing to send forth another hoot.

He greeted her. "It is good to see that you have survived. After I lost sight of you during the chaos I was concerned."

"I was fine. It seemed prudent to cast a sheath of invisibility and leave."

"Do you know what happened to Draag? The last I saw of him he was filling the hall with flame. I had to dive through a window to evade one such blast."

Tallenna smiled a bitter smile. "The last I saw of him, he was outside in the street looking for the girl who'd spurned his offer of congress."

"I sometimes wonder why we are with him."

"I also. There are many things in this world that make little sense, and this is one of them."

Yann looked to be still thinking of a reply when Hill, Shovel, and the monkey crashed out of the undergrowth and skidded to a half in front of Yann and Tallenna.

"What the hell happened back there?"

Yann and Tallenna answered in unison. "Draag."

"You hear a noise coming from the forest," the AllFather tells them. "Someone approaching. A figure appears at the edge of the clearing."

He nods at the Warrior.

The Warrior puffs out his chest. "You need wait no more. Draag has returned. Let us continue our quest for glory and riches. Let us march!"

"March where?" chorus three voices.

Draag spun round and pointed in what looked suspiciously to Yann like a random direction.

"This way!"

Yann called upon his inner voice to grant him calm and serenity. "Why that way?"

Draag advanced menacingly towards him, pomp, stench and fury in equal measures. "Do you have a better idea of which way to go?"

"Well, no!" snapped Yann, still waiting for his inner voice to arrive. "But whose damned fault is that?"

"Three days you spent in that bloody village and what did you find out? Would I be right if I surmised the answer was nothing?"

Yann felt his hand going for his quarterstaff. Where he had sought his inner voice he found only images of gentle people engulfed in flame and touched with death.

A glowing purple wall appeared in front of him, a ghostly Draag barely visible through its opaque surface. Tallenna's voice cut across the clearing.

"We have a duty to perform, and fighting among ourselves won't achieve that. No matter how justified."

Yann took a step back and the force wall disappeared. Tallenna walked over to him, took his arm, and led him away.

"We need you Yann. The worse Draag's actions, the more we need you." She smiled. "Come on. For what it's worth, I think Draag's direction is as good as any other. Let's march."

The OverRealm. What passes for later.

The AllFather has no watch to examine to monitor the passing of time, nor time to monitor. As mentioned several times already, time has no meaning in this realm, and not surprisingly, watches have no meaning either.

But in the mortal realms that the AllFather has created, time does have a meaning and, that being so, some of the more enterprising of his creations have devised devices that track the passing of that time. The more fashionable among the more enterprising have taken this further: they have attached the devices to their wrists. They claim – to themselves, their friends, and to anyone they can corner at a party – that this is so that they can learn of the current time with only a moment's movement and glance.

This is, of course, a lie. Having been clever enough to construct such intricate devices of clockwork and magic, they are then vain enough to strap them to their wrists in order that all might be witness to their cleverness.

And upon doing so all around them do indeed acknowledge their cleverness; and several months later, when they destroy their intricate device of magic and clockwork with one careless swing of the arm, all around them acknowledge (behind their backs) the stupidity with which cleverness is so often paired.

None of this is relevant except for one detail: right now the

AllFather wishes he did have a watch to examine, if only to prove to himself that existence is still existing, something which he is rapidly starting to doubt.

The table is silent, and inspiration appears to be in short supply.

"Perhaps we should just recap where we are," the AllFather suggests. "You were travelling though the forest on the bearing suggested by the Warrior when you heard the sound of hooves from a little way in front of you. This then led onto a debate on what actions should be taken next."

"Which then devolved into another discussion on the subject of the village," adds the Lady.

"Yes. Perhaps if we got back onto the subject of the sound of hooves?"

A series of uneasily glances are swapped around the table. Finally, the clearly unhappy Dealer speaks, wearily.

"I still say that we should go and meet whoever or whatever it is."

The Warrior shrugs. "Fine. It's your funeral, not that I'll be attending it."

The road ran broad and true through the forest, climbing gently up the slope of the ridge to disappear over the crest, its polished marble surface giving no clue as to its age. Yann halted somewhere near the road's centreline and turned to face the sound of approaching hooves.

Two men came into view, riding on white steeds that were horselike save for the two white horns each sported. As the men approached he saw that they were Weshens. The wheeled their mounts to a halt a little way from him, and hailed him.

"Greetings, stranger!" called the older-looking of the pair. "We have been searching for you."

"I'll take out the one on the right with DeathSinger's flamejet," the Warrior tells the Dealer. "You take out the one on the left."

Yann slowly waved his hand at the older-looking Weshen and began to speak, getting as far as "Greetings to you–" before Draag's booming shout of "I'll take out the one on the right with DeathSinger's flamejet, you take out the one on the left!" echoed through the forest.

The Warrior leans as far forward as the table's edge will allow him, and shakes his fist at the AllFather. "That was me saying that, not Draag, and you know it!"

The AllFather holds out a hand, trying to calm the situation. "But it was an instruction from Draag to Yann instructing Yann what he should do. And since Yann is standing in the middle of the road, and Draag's thirty feet away in the forest, you'd have to raise your voice in order that he can hear you."

"Yann is right!" said a solemn Hill. "We cannot simply leave like this. If Stone is indeed lost to us, then we must remember him appropriately."

Yann thought for a moment, and then nodded. "I know not of the customs of Stone's people when remembering fallen colleagues. What know you?"

"Search me!" exclaims the Jester. He looks over at the Sleeper. "What customs do Stone's people have for this sort of thing?"
"Customs?" says the Sleeper, confused. "People?"
"Where does he come from?" the Lady asks.
"The Known Lands. That's where they all come from, isn't it? Was I supposed to pick a specific area?"

The halfling shrugged, sadly. "I know not of his people's customs either. Perhaps I could lead us through the ceremony of remembrance that my people use to remember the fallen and the lost?"

Yann stepped towards the halfling, and knelt down to look him in the eye. "Though you are small in stature you are mighty in spirit. I, Yann, son of Yonna who was daughter of Yakka, of the clan Grell and the Northern Plains, am pleased to call you a brother. Please, continue, and lead us in your people's ways."

The halfling said nothing, but instead went to his saddlebags, extracting four small tin cups, and a bottle containing an amber coloured fluid.

He poured a small quantity of the fluid into each cup, handing one to each of his three colleagues and keeping one for himself.

"The fire of this drink represents the fire of the life of the one we are remembering. We now stand facing each other, and raise our cups."

Hill stood before Yann, with Tallenna to his left, and Draag to his right.

"To Stone!" he called, holding his cup in front of him.

"To Stone!" the others echoed.

Hill threw the cup of liquid down his throat. It burned agreeably, as it should have done; he had, after all, liberated it from the lowest sections of the Wesh village's wine cellars.

He looked slowly around each of this three colleagues, and nodded.

"Okay. Let's go!"

"You call that a memorial?" the Dealer asks.
The Jester shrugs. "Works for me."
A voice breaks in from across the table.
It is the Sleeper. "Aren't memorials something you do for dead people?"
No-one answers him.
"I can't be dead," he says. He looks at the AllFather. "You'd have

said if I was dead! You didn't, did you?"

"No I didn't," the AllFather tells him. "You're not dead." He looks at each of the other Gods in turn. "You didn't have a memorial service at the time, so you can't go back and say you had one now. I've already said that we're having no more time wind-backs. Doing so makes a mockery of the entire mortal realm. From now on, what happens, happens, and you'll just have to deal with the consequences."

He pauses for a moment, then holds up his hands. "Why, if we were going to wind time back to when you met up in the clearing, then we might as well wind it back another hour or so to before Draag entered the village and before you lost Stone, and thus get rid of this entire problem!"

"I find that acceptable!" proclaims the Warrior.

"Works for me too!" adds the Jester.

"It would solve many difficulties," the Dealer admits reluctantly.

The Lady nods in agreement.

The Jester leans forward. "So, the village then?"

"But you didn't bother to mention that she didn't want to do it!"

"Why would I say that, when it's surely obvious to all that she wouldn't be willing!"

"Why would she not be willing?" the Warrior exclaims.

"Because you're a pig?" the Lady suggests.

"Because you've just spent four days lying in mud pissing and shitting yourself and as a result smell worse than a pig farm suffering from a dysentery epidemic?" the Jester adds.

"Because she is the daughter of a pure and noble culture while you are a sworn servant of evil?" says the Dealer.

The Warrior considers this for a moment. "No, I'm sorry. This still doesn't make sense. She's still a woman. She will still be drawn to the power of a warrior."

"I think you'll find you might be mistaken," says the Lady.

Yann stood before Draag, too furious to speak.

Draag leaned forward and lowered his voice. "And I was rather, you know, otherwise engaged."

Yann continued glaring at him.

"Perhaps you could come back later?"

Still Yann said nothing, every iota of his being concentrating on not beating Draag to a bloody pulp.

"Yann?"

Glare.

"You okay?"

Glare.

Finally, some glimmer of understanding, perhaps combined with some instinct of self-preservation, appeared to penetrate Draag's brain. He looked back through the doorway.

"Do you actually want to do it?

A sob emerged from the room.

"Really?" Draag asked, a puzzled frown on his face. "Are you sure?"

Another sob emerged.

"Oh well," said Draag, shrugging. "I'll never understand women."

He stood aside as the sobbing Weshen girl run past him and down the corridor, clutching the torn remains of her robes to her chest."

Draag watched her go, then turned his attention back to Yann.

"So what was it you wanted?"

"It is the next morning. Aides have helped you wash–"

The Jester points at the Warrior, grinning, and opens his mouth to speak, but is silenced by a glare from the AllFather.

"–and have dressed you in magnificent costumes that fit you better than any clothing you've ever worn. They have taken you to a

51

marbled terrace that sits before a vista that quite literally takes your breath away and have served you a breakfast of honeyed bread and exotic fruits and tea that dances on the palate."

"I'm more a coffee man, myself," mutters the Jester.

"Shut up! Anyway, once you have finished eating—"

"I didn't say I was eating!" protests the Warrior, angrily.

"You don't want to eat breakfast?" the AllFather asks warily.

"It's not about whether or not I breakfast!"

The Jester puts on a an implausibly innocent face. "You wanted cereal?"

"It is not about what food is on offer!" says the Warrior, assuming an offended pose. "I do not think that it is right for you to railroad us like this!"

"Assuming that you would eat breakfast," says the AllFather, carefully, "is railroading you?"

"You are not supposed to tell us what our mortals do. You are supposed to ask us what we want our mortals to do."

"Fine," the AllFather snaps. "An aide – a male aide! – enters your room and tells you that he has come to help you bathe and dress and will then escort you to breakfast."

The AllFather takes a deep breath.

"What do you want to do?"

"I will let him run the bath and arrange my clothes, but I'm am a warrior, and will bathe and dress myself."

"Fine. Do you come to breakfast?"

"Yes!"

"Thank you. As I was saying, after breakfasting on honeyed bread and exotic fruits—"

"I did not want fruit!"

The Jester holds his head in his hands. "In the name of everything that ever was and ever shall be, can we please, please, just get past breakfast?"

"It is a point of principle. I shall not be railroaded."

The AllFather holds up a hand. "Can we at least agree that you have arrived at the breakfast table?"

The Warrior nods. "We can agree on that. I have arrived at the breakfast table."

"Good. You are sat around a large oak breakfast table that stands on a terrace outside the palace. The table's huge surface is filled with a dazzling array of breads, sauces, spreads, and uncountable types of exotic fruit. Beyond the terrace, the ground descends through a series of drops to the valley below, forming a vista so magnificent that your breath is quite literally—"

"I think we can take the general magnificence of the view as noted, and proceed."

The AllFather glares at him. "Fine. You are sitting at the table. What do you want to do?"

The Jester leans forward. "I'll pick up a small loaf or roll in my left hand, pick up a knife in my right hand, and then using a rhythmic back-and-forth movement slice the loaf or roll into two halves. I will then start scanning the table to see what spreads are available. Is there any marmalade or similarly orange coloured spread?"

The Warrior leans as far across the table as he can. "Are you mocking me?"

The AllFather breaks into the resulting shouting match. "Can we just assume that you all eat breakfast?"

"I want some meat. Draag is not a vegetarian and he shall not breakfast on fruit."

The Weshen head aide took a stumbled step back, so great was the horror of what had been suggested to him.

"You want... Meat? The dead flesh of a slaughtered animal, roasted?"

"I think grilled might do," suggested Hill with a chuckle. He splattered a bit more marmalade onto a fruit loaf, arranging the spread just so. "I'd be up for a bacon sandwich myself, if that was on offer."

The Weshen head aide regained some control. "We live our lives by a number of simple principles, one of which is to live in peace and harmony with our fellow creatures. We do not kill them, we do not eat them. Surely you learned this during your stay in the village?"

"He spent that time lying in a corn field."

"But you were there for four days?"

"Don't ask. Really. Trust me on this one."

Draag banged the table, picked up a heavy looking knife, and banged the table once more. "I am a warrior. I demand meat for my breakfast."

"This is ridiculous!"

"No it's not," the AllFather protests. "The Wesh are a pure and noble people against which men are mere children. They have moved beyond the ways of the flesh."

"It's not that unusual," the Jester adds helpfully. "It's quite common for elves to be vegetarians!"

"They're not elves!"

"Are you sure?"

"I am the Lord of all Creation. I am he who took the dust and shaped it into reality. I am the bringer of life and the bringer of death. I think I'd know if they were elves or not, and I'm telling you that they're not!"

"Well, if you're sure?"

"I am!"

"I was just trying to be helpful," the Jester mutters.

Silence descends.

Eventually the Dealer speaks. "Is there any chance of us getting past breakfast?"

53

The head aide waved a hand, and a host of Weshen materialised from a concealed doorway. Within moments, they'd efficiently removed the remains of the breakfast feast.

The aide waited until the table was clear, and then spoke. "In due course our priest of priests will brief you on the mission we have called you here to perform. Until then, I am at your service to act as your guide around our world. What would you like to see?

> "I want to test myself against their mightiest warriors!"
> "I'd like to visit their library, and perhaps talk with their mages and scholars."
> "I'd like to talk with their priests and learn something of their ways."
> "Have they got a basement?"
> "Warriors?"
> "Order must be maintained somehow!"
> "Why?"
> "Or perhaps some kind of tunnel system?"
> The AllFather holds up a hand, which is ignored until he follows it up with a snapped, "Be quiet! All of you!"
> Silence resumes, somewhat grudgingly.
> "Thank you."

"But you are brothers-in-arms, comrades who have fought through terrible challenges and survived; a group forged in battle, and tempered by long and arduous journeys. I would have thought you would wish to stay together, and see our realm as one group?"

> "Don't try and justify this," the Warrior snaps. "You're just trying to make things simpler for yourself."
> "Well I was actually trying to make things simpler for all of us. But fine, if that's what you want."

Nunna had trained for this task for more than a thousand years, and yet he still had to think for a moment. This was not an eventuality he had expected. But neither was it one for which he was completely unprepared. He clapped his hands together, and five younger Weshens appeared from the hidden doorway.

He called them over one by one.

"Oklarer!" The young female nodded respectfully. "You shall go with Yann. He wishes to talk with our priests and learn of our ways."

The Northlander thanked him, and departed with his guide.

"Alaqa!" A young male – rumour or truth, he'd made sure of that – strode confidently over. The aide noted the dark paladin's scowl, but ignored it.

"Yes!" the Priest of Priests snaps. "I am going to explain what is going on and you are going to listen to me. Are you going to sit there and listen or would you rather sit outside and leave your comrades to hear what I have to say?"

The Jester holds his head in his hands as the Dealer waves an angry finger in the brooding Warrior's face.
"Leave it! Just leave it!"
"Draag is a sworn paladin of darkness! He would not accept such an insult!"
"Not even from the King of the Elves?"
The AllFather starts to protest, but then gives up, saying: "Oh what's the point?"
The Warrior picks up the knuckle-bones and gives them a slow shake.
"Draag would not accept this."

To the end of his days, Yann would swear that he had not even seen the old Weshen move. Yann was trained in the ancient ways of his shaman ancestors. He could sense time, could slice it, could sense the progress of an eyelid across the eye.

But now his eyes had missed the transition from frail and seated old man to furious standing mage, had missed the beams of raw energy emerging from the mage's outstretched fingers, had missed the raw energy binding a thousand tangled webs around Draag before the paladin had an instant to move.

"That's not fair! We did not cast the knuckle-bones to determine who would react first!"
The AllFather holds up a placating hand. "You are correct. We should have done so. Please go ahead."
The Warrior gives his knuckle-bones a final shake and throws them across the table.
"Five successes!"
The AllFather nods. He picks up the knuckle-bones that lay before him, pauses for a moment, then turns to first the Lady, and then the Jester, and asks: "Do you mind?" At their nods, he picks up the sets of knuckle-bones that lay before each of them.
Then he casts them across the table.
"Thirty-seven successes," he announces, calmly.

To the end of his days, Yann would swear that he had not even seen the old Weshen move. Yann was trained in the ancient ways of his shaman ancestors. He could sense time, could slice it, could sense the progress of an eyelid across the eye.

But now his eyes had missed the transition from frail and seated old man to furious standing mage, had missed the beams of raw energy emerging from the mage's outstretched fingers, had missed the raw energy binding a thousand tangled webs around Draag before the paladin had an instant to move.

"Thirty seven successes?" the Warrior exclaims. "That is not possible!"

The AllFather shrugs. "He is old beyond time and the possessor of knowledge beyond the comprehension of the human realms from which your mortals have come. He is capable of such acts."

"Perhaps," the Warrior mutters. "I have my suspicions as to how long he has been capable of such acts though!"

"What do you mean?" the Lady asks.

The Warrior waves an angry hand. "Well he's making this up as he goes along, isn't he?"

"That is completely untrue," the AllFather insists, successfully resisting the temptation to look down at his tablets and re-read the words describing the Priests of Priests that are scribed upon them.

They are only notes, he tells himself. Nothing exists until I will it into reality.

"Of course," say the Warrior unhappily. He crosses his arms and glares at a spot on the wall.

The Priest of Priests waited until the bound and gagged paladin of darkness had given up his furious attempts to escape his bonds, and then resumed speaking.

"For hundreds of thousands of what you call years we lived upon this world, both this side of the central mountain ridge, and the other, the realms where men now live."

The halfling coughed discretely into his fist.

"And halflings," the Priest of Priests added.

He took a moment to gather his thoughts, and then continued. "But over time though, we grew curious about the world. We travelled north, to where the world is eternally frozen, and south to where there is only endless burning desert. We used our magic to drill deep into the rock below us, and to fly high into the sky above us. For tens of millennia we explored, and for tens of millennia more we sought to understand what we had found."

He paused, unsure how to continue. Eventually, the Northlander raised a hand, and at the Priest of Priest's nod, spoke.

"What did you find?"

The old Weshen paused once more, and sighed. Finally, he found the words, poor as they were.

"We found that the world was mortally sick, and would shortly die. The land would tear into a thousand million pieces and sink into the sea. A mighty cataclysm that would destroy everyone and everything."

He had expected questions then, but got only stunned and horrified silence. Finally though, the Northlander spoke once more.

"You say that you found that the world would shortly be destroyed. When did you find this out?"

"Some eighteen thousand of your years ago."

"So how come we're not dead then?" asked the halfling.

"Because to them, shortly has a totally different meaning than it does to humans," the AllFather explains. "His use of the word shortly to talk about something that is more than eighteen thousand years away illustrates that."

"Right..." the Jester replies, clearly not convinced.

"So why didn't you do something when you realised?" the Northlander asked cautiously.

"We did do something," the Priest of Priests told him. "We created you."

"You created us? Why?"

"Because only you could heal the world and prevent the cataclysm. For reasons that I will soon explain, we, the Wesh, could not. And so we created you, the race of men, in order that you, in time, would become capable of preventing the death of the world. In a sense, you are our children. And having given birth to you, we retreated to this side of the world and built the Wall, in order that you would have the time and space you needed to mature as a race."

The Northlander thought for a moment. "And the purpose of the Gate, and the Riddle, was to judge the moment when we had matured enough?"

The Priest of Priests nodded, happy that his teaching session was back on track. "Exactly."

There was a silence, and then the halfling spoke. "You keep on saying about how you created men in order to save the world. What about us halflings?"

Ah, the Priest of Priests thought. Bugger. He coughed, embarrassed. "Well there were some preliminary experiments..."

"Oh that's just great," the Jester exclaims. "I'm a failed prototype!"

"Well I wouldn't describe the situation quite like that," says the AllFather.

"Well how would you describe it?" says the Jester bitterly.

"You're the one who insisted on creating a halfling mortal," says the Lady. "Even though we were all supposed to be creating men."

"That is true," says the AllFather hurriedly. "That did force me to adjust things somewhat."

"Oh well I'm sorry for disrupting your cosmology!" shouts the Jester.

"Well I don't see what your problem is!" exclaims the Lady. "You created a joke character: a tall halfling with a part-terrier riding dog. Why should you care about one more joke?"

The Jester extends a bitter finger at the AllFather. "Because it's his joke, not mine."

"Perhaps you should have played a midget?" the Warrior suggests.

The Northlander raised his hand once more, and spoke. "You say that the world is going to be destroyed, but you have not explained how or why this is going to happen?"

The Priest of Priests sighed. "I have not, but that is because first I must explain to you what we found when we explored the world."

He stood painfully up from his chair, and waved toward a black door set into the far wall of the meeting room.

"Come with me."

The room they entered was dark save for the lit plinth that lay at its centre, but some factor of its design reminded Tallenna of the great Observatory Dome built atop the Institute's highest tower.

The old Weshen motioned them to stand before the plinth, then waved a hand in a purposeful manner.

In an instant, the plain surface of the plinth was filled with a perfect model of the palace and the landscape around it. He waved his hand once more, and the model grew, until they were looking at the terrace upon which they had that morning eaten breakfast.

"It's an image, of this building?" Yann asked in wonder. "As though we were flying above it?"

"It is," said the old priest.

Yann stepped forward, to examine the model. He peered for a moment, then pointed at the terrace. "This is not how it is now. The stones in this are less worn."

"That is so, child of my people. This does not show this palace as it is now, but as it was eighteen thousand years ago."

He paused for a moment, and then spoke once more, his voice now heavy, as though weighted with the responsibility of what he was to say – or was it guilt?

"Before I continue, I must warn you. I am about to reveal a truth of such enormity that I have spent the last eighteen thousand years struggling to comprehend it, and struggle still. All exposed to this truth have so struggled, a struggle that some lost. Some still battle the madness that this truth has bought them."

He walked along the line they formed, stopping in front of each one to offer a hand on the shoulder, or an empathic glance.

"Am I still bound and gagged or what?"
"Are you going to try and kill him?"
"No."
"Then he cancelled the spell before you came here."

"Though the fate of the world rests upon your shoulders–"

"That's not actually true," says the Jester. "Other groups could answer the riddle and come–"
"Draag killed the Gatekeeper," the Dealer points out.
"Oh yeah. Guess we'd better listen to what the old guy's saying then."
"Could you?" the AllFather asks acidly.

"–I cannot ask that you witness this, for no-one has the right to ask someone to learn a truth of such enormity that their sanity might be crushed as a result. If any of you wish to leave, then leave now."

Tallenna did not leave. Nor, she saw, did any of her four comrades.

Finally, the old man resumed speaking.

"For thousands upon thousands of years the world had been static and unchanging. We had assumed it to be eternal, and so thought not of it, devoting our energies to the study of ourselves."

"Is it me, or are elves always total narcissists?" asks the Jester.
"Shut up!" the AllFather tells him. "For once, please, just shut up!"

"Then the world started changing." The Priest of Priests waved his hand and the image on the plinth changed to a view of a volcano, lava pouring from vents across its flanks. "The very land started to rip and tear, and the molten rock that should lie in the world's heart started pouring out. These changes concerned us, scared us, and we started to realise how little we understood of the world upon which we lived."

He waved his hand again, and the plinth's image changed to a view of a pastoral landscape from above, the trees and hills below tiny and perfect. For an instant it stayed so, and then the viewpoint dived towards the ground.

Tallenna felt herself gasp. Her mind knew it was only an image; but it was so real.

They hit the ground, but continued, as though flying through rock that changed colour and shade until finally it was glowing red and flowing.

"We used our magic to drill down into the ground, but that gave us no answers."

He waved his hand once more, and the plinth's image changed back to the view of the landscape. For an instant, it stayed still. Then the viewpoint started to rise, slowly. The trees grew tiny, became dots, and then specks. Soon they could see a whole region, thread-like rivers meandering through valleys shrunk to mere grooves.

"We had flown high before, but now we flew higher than we ever had. Higher than the birds. Higher than the clouds. So high that the air first grew cold, and then ceased to be. So high that we had to develop new magic that we might survive in such a place. Higher and higher we flew."

He waved his hand, and the rate of climb increased. The land displayed on the plinth shrank and shrank and shrank.

"Higher and higher until the truth of the world was revealed."

Finally the image's climb stopped.

Tallenna struggled to comprehend what she was seeing.

An endless ocean that stretched to the very ends of the Universe.

And swimming through that sea, endlessly chasing the southern sun, shrouded in blue sky and enveloped in clouds, a lizard – no a sea serpent! – that her mind told her must be more than thirty thousand miles long and that her soul told her could not possibly be.

Seconds, minutes, passed by, as they watched the beast that was the world swim through the ocean that was the universe. The bony ridge along its back: the mountain range that split the world. Its flanks: the coasts. Each lazy roll from side to side: a tide.

Finally, Hill let out an awed sigh.

The old Weshen spoke. "You are overwhelmed, are you not?"

Hill nodded. "I am. It's just so..."

He paused clearly struggling for words, and then took a deep breath.

"Wank."

The OverRealm. Footsteps echo away down the hallway from behind the recently slammed door.

The five figures who remain at the table look at each other.

"That wasn't very nice," says the Lady, icily, staring hard at the Jester.

"Oh come on," he protests, holding his hands up beside him. "A giant sea serpent so big it's got soil and trees and people living on it! You don't think that's just a bit cheesy?"

The Lady shrugs, embarrassed. "I think it's got a certain charm."

"Meaning you think it's crap too, but you're too polite to say so!"

The Jester looks around the table for support, finally stopping on the Warrior who, after a pause speaks.

"Could I point out for the record, that this was his fault, not mine."

"Thanks."

The Warrior shrugs, uncaring. "So how long do you think this sulk's going to last?" he asks.

"You uncaring bastards!" the Lady exclaims. "Do you have any idea how long it took him to create his world?"

"More than six days?" suggests the Jester.

The Lady ignores him. "Do you have any idea how hard he worked? He started with dust!"

The Warrior sighs. "Here she goes again," he mutters.

"What's that supposed to mean?"

The Warrior puts out his hands in what he intends as a placatory gesture. "I mean no insult Mistress Lady. You are simply being what your nature compels you to be."

"Exactly!" adds the Jester. "You are, after all, the mistress of man's despair."

The Lady takes a deep breath before speaking, and when she does her voice is slow and controlled. "And why am I the mistress of man's despair?"

She looks around table, but receives only four apologetic shrugs in reply.

"Because you pigs jumped in and grabbed all the decent realms before I had a chance to open my mouth. Even the bloody dog got a better job than me!"

Beneath the table, the Dog, Lord of Man's Loyalty, stirs at the mention of his name. His tail thumps against the marble floor.

The Dealer clears his throat. "Despair isn't that bad a realm to have."

"That's easy for you to say!" the Lady spits back. "You got contentment!"

The Dealer waves his hands as he tries to shape his words. "Well we thought that despair would be a good realm for you to have," he says, looking at first the Warrior, and then the Jester, getting eager nods in return. "What with you being a woman."

The OverRealm. Footsteps echo away down the hallway from behind the now twice-slammed door.

The four figures remaining at the table look at each other.

"Women!" ventures the Warrior finally.

Silence descends.

"Game of knuckle-bones?" he suggests.

Chapter Nine

The OverRealm. The Warrior has been playing knuckle-bones for a little over what, in the mortal realm, would be termed "half an hour" and though, as frequently mentioned, time has no meaning here, he has none the less been playing long enough to have gambled away the Determination, Enterprise and Initiative aspects of his domain.

He picks up the knuckle-bones in front of him, shakes them hard, and casts them out across the table.

"Damn it all!" he shouts.

The Dealer speaks. "I believe that gives Eagerness to me, Lord Warrior."

"I think you'll find he's only the Lord of Would-Quite-Like-To-Do-Something now," says the Jester, chucking.

One of the disadvantages of living in a realm where time, not having any meaning, has no jurisdiction either, is that most conventional excuses for exiting a game of chance – mealtime, toilet break, latest episode of favourite soap about to start – do not apply.

Even if these excuses were applicable though, the Warrior would not make them, for is he not the Warrior, Lord of at least part of Man's Ambition?

He picks up the knuckle-bones, and glares at his fellow gods. "I am still the Lord of Motivation, Resolve, Zeal and Commitment!" He pauses, shakes once, pauses again, shakes twice, pauses, and then sends the knuckle-bones dancing across the table.

"Damnation!"

Three casts, two losses and one bout of cursing later, a figure appears at the door. It is the AllFather.

"I see you found something to occupy yourselves with while I was gone," he says, a little coldly.

The Sleeper looks at him in confusion. He opens his hands to show the knuckle-bones he is about to cast. "We were playing knuckle-bones," he says. "I think I'm now the Lord of Resolve, Chance and something else!"

"Satisfaction," says the Jester. The Dealer sends an evil glance his way, to which the Jester merely shrugs.

"Satisfaction! That's it! And what were the other two?"

The AllFather sits down and picks up his tablets. He has often noted that the mortals in his realm are driven to prayer, and has wondered what it is that drives them so. Now he knows; he'd pray right now if it weren't for the fact that he's the one who'd have to listen.

He looks around the table. "Where's Mistress Lady?"

The Dealer coughs. "She left."

The Jester and the Warrior nod.

"Why?"

The Jester, the Warrior, and the Dealer shrug in unison.

"We could go on without her," the Warrior suggests. He looks at the Dealer, who looks away, uneasy, and at the Jester, who provides another all-purpose shrug.

The AllFather considers this for a moment, and for that moment is tempted, until the possible consequences dawn.

The creator of the entire universe stifles an embarrassed cough.

"Perhaps we'd better do something else until she comes back."

The battle had been raging for only thirty minutes, but things were already looking bleak. An urgent synthetic voice erupted from the cockpit speakers of Redd Jansen's Sunfire Mk V starfighter.

"Break left! Break left!"

He slammed the sidestick as far left as it would go and felt his damaged ship roll in response, slowly, too slowly. A vacuum-silenced spray of laser bolts stitched through the space where he'd been mere moments before.

He thumbed the side-stick's transmit button and began screaming orders: "Red Squadron! This is Red Leader! Form up on my tail and–"

"I see you found something to do then," observes the Lady, returning to the room.

The AllFather looks up, embarrassed, caught in the act of pushing a small but perfect model across the table.

"We weren't sure when you were coming back," he explains. "I don't think we were quite sure why you went, actually."

She looks slowly around the table.

"Were we not? Well I'm here now, so perhaps you can all put your little toys away and we can resume."

After the longest second of Yann's life, the old Weshen spoke. "Well we all thought it was pretty awesome, even if you don't."

"No, no," said Hill from beside Yann, seriousness written across his face. "It was incredible. Awesome. I mean, a giant sea serpent thirty thousand miles long – who'd've thunk it?"

The AllFather angrily pushes his chair back and stands. "Look, if you're just going to carry on making fun I'm going to stop bothering!"

"Who's making fun?" the Jester protests.

The Lady glares at him, and then puts a hand on the AllFather's arm. "Just ignore him. I think it's very creative, myself."

Tallenna had not yet spoken, was still struggling to comprehend the enormity of the truths just revealed. Calm, she told herself. You always knew you were a speck of dust in an infinite universe. That speck is still the same even if the universe is not.

She stepped forward.

"I, Tallenna, child, apprentice, graduate and fellow of the Institute of Magic thank you for revealing to us a truth so eternal and fundamental."

"I Yann, son of Yonna who was daughter of –"

"Yadda, yadda, yadda," says the Warrior. He strikes a pose and begins to speak.

"I Draag, paladin–"

"I was speaking!" protests the Dealer.

"Look we've heard it all before so I think we can take it as read."

"I Draag–"

"No, you look! Yann is a plains barbarian. He derives his status and self-worth not from land or from possessions but from linage and reputation. This is important to him."

The Jester chuckles. "The elf's over twenty thousand years old. Perhaps Lord Warrior is worried he'll die of old age while waiting for you to recite your family tree."

The AllFather says nothing, and successfully resists the temptation to give the Priest of Priests an immediate seizure followed by death. He waits until a sulky silence settles upon the table and then speaks.

"Have we all finished? Then I think it was Lord Dealer's turn to speak."

"I Yann–"

"What's yadda, yadda, yadda mean, anyhow?" asks the Jester.

"I'm not entirely sure," replies the Warrior. "I heard Mr Six Day's son use it once in conversation. I think it means shut up, you're boring me."

"Right, that's it!" shouts the AllFather. "I didn't want to have to do this, but you've given me no option!" He stands up, and walks over to an alcove set in the wall, within which is placed an iridescent shell that shines like a thousand rainbows. "From now on, you can only speak if you have the conch."

He slides it across the table to the Dealer.

"I Yann–"

"I have a question," says the Warrior, interrupting.

"You cannot speak!" shouts the Dealer, waving the shell he

clutches in his hand. "You do not have the conch!"

"But Lord Warrior is making a point of order," says the Jester.

"Well, yes," says the Warrior. He thinks for a moment, then smiles at the Jester "Yes. Yes I am!"

"And besides," adds the Jester, "surely possession of the conch merely indicates the right for your mortal to speak. It doesn't mean that we ourselves have to remain mute, surely? If that were so, then it would mean that while the conch holder's mortal was speaking, we would not even be able to command our mortals to move. It can only refer to our mortals taking turns to speak."

"I suppose so," says the AllFather uneasily. "What's your question?" he asks the Warrior.

"I was going to ask whether or not we ourselves needed the conch in order to speak."

The Jester butts in with a cackle. "Which you've now answered by allowing him to ask the question!"

"This is pitiful!" shouts the Lady. "If you all just stop bickering like a bunch of mortal children we might actually find out what it is our mortals are supposed to be doing and start doing some actual epic questing!"

She casts a glare across each one of them.

"Okay?"

Five heads frantically nod.

Tallenna stepped forward once more, past the clearly overawed Yann, and spoke in the clear controlled voice that her mage-mentors had taught her.

"Tell us, wise one: how can we who have answered your call prevent the world-serpent from dying?"

"But I've got the conch!" says the Dealer, hurt.

The Lady shoots him the look she uses when men's souls need flaying.

The Dealer mouths a silent "okay", and puts the conch down.

The AllFather goes to speak, thinks better of it, and glances nervously at the Lady. She sighs, raises her eyebrows and then nods. He continues.

"Now, can you all remember where the Priest of Priests had got to in his explanation?"

The Sleeper leans forward. "I remember he said something about volcanoes, but I didn't quite catch the bit that came after that. What was it he said?"

"How? Well we had watched as the earth began to tear, and molten rock began to pour from those tears. It was not until we realised the true nature of the world that we realised that the earth was skin, the tears were wounds, and the lava was blood. Our most skilled healers and herbalists devoted themselves to this problem, both by studying the world, and by studying its smaller reptile cousins that dwell upon its surface."

Tallenna thought for a moment. "It's going to shed its skin!"

"Exactly. It will renew its skin in the same way that all reptiles do, by shedding the old skin to reveal the new beneath. It will live on."

"But we won't," said Yann.

"No."

"But you said there is a way we can stop this," said Tallenna.

"There is. After thousands of years of study, our herbalists developed a healing elixir which will renew and revitalise the existing skin and thus prevent it shedding. Your task is to apply that elixir."

"But why can your people not do that?" asked Yann, confused. "What is so special about we men?"

Tallenna coughed.

"And women."

Hill coughed.

"And halflings."

The old Weshen paused. "We Weshens are a highly empathic people. We sense emotions and thoughts and desires. The world-serpent's thoughts would burn our minds to an empty shell. That is why we created you, you whose empathic sensing is almost nil."

"But I don't understand," said Tallenna. "You stand on the surface of the world-serpent now, unharmed."

"Of course, but this is not where the elixir must be applied."

"Well where do we have to go to apply it?" asked Yann.

"Why to the head of course!"

Chapter Ten

Kallie would have been an attractive little girl were it not for the dirt on her face and the rags she wore. She was ten, and had been fending for herself in the City's winding streets and dark alleyways for as long as she could recall.

In all those years she'd seen many strange and wondrous things. This was the City, after all, the largest, richest, most advanced and most cosmopolitan settlement on the surface of the World. As the people of the City were wont to tell others: "If we don't have it, no-one will."

Kallie had seen wizards and elephants and magical horseless carriages and men riding dragons and staffs that spat fire – but she had never seen anything like what came swooping down towards her as she sat on her haunches sorting through the morning's rubbish in the Lord High Mayor's personal tip.

At first, when it was little more than a speck in the sky, she'd thought it a bird; certainly, as it got closer, it proved to have wings that beat at the air with a rhythmic hum.

But as it descended, and turned – it was landing she realised! – she saw that it was a ship, crafted from wood and metal, with men – and a woman! – and a halfling! – riding atop it, looking down at her with slightly frightened eyes.

And at the front, face set in concentration, was the man who controlled the giant mechanical bird – but he was strange. Tall. And thin. With silver hair.

And pointed ears.

The strange craft landed. Kallie watched as its even stranger pilot climbed down from his ship and stood beside it, looking around, and noticing her. What she was now seeing was beyond any abilities of comprehension she'd accumulated in her short and hard life. She did not understand what she was seeing. Could not.

But she nonetheless knew what she had to do.

She walked over to the strange pilot and set herself squarely before him, hands on hips, looking up at his tall figure.

"Five silver crowns to watch over your ship and make sure nothing bad happens to it mister!" she told him. "Wouldn't want it to get all scratched, would we?"

"Five silver crowns!" exclaims the Jester. "Either the City's just suffered a bout of massive inflation or that's one street urchin with enough cheek for an entire street gang!"

"Are you going to sit up there whining?" asks the AllFather, "or are you going to do something?"

71

"I'll climb down and let the animals out of the hold."

"Fine. You do that. Your dog's a bit upset and the monkey's not that happy either. What are the rest of you doing?"

"I'll stay here," says the Dealer. "I'm not sure why we came here anyway."

"I am forced to agree," says the Warrior. "We have a mission to perform. I do not understand why Mistress Lady and Lord Jester were so adamant that we make this diversion."

The Lady ignores both of them, and instead speaks directly to the AllFather.

"I'll climb down and talk to the little girl."

Tallenna stepped down from the last of the footholds carved into the ornithopter's sheer side and crouched down in front of the little girl.

"Hello! My name's Tallenna. What's yours?"

"Kallie," the little girl replied. "And you can talk to me as nicely as you like but the price's still five silver crowns."

Hill's voice emerged from the open cargo hold. "That's daylight robbery. She can have two copper crowns and that's that."

"Don't worry about my friend," said Tallenna. "He can be a bit gruff at times but his heart's in the right place."

Hill's head popped around the open doorway. "You'd be gruff if you'd seen the state of this cargo hold."

The AllFather looks across at the Jester and speaks quietly. "Make a dodge test."

"Why?"

"Because there's a piece of monkey poo heading your way."

"Oh nice," says the Jester sarcastically, picking up his knuckle-bones and shaking them in his cupped hands. "This was just the sort of high adventure I was looking for."

He casts them across the table.

"Dammit!"

Hill had always prided himself on being a quick learner, and in the thirty seconds that had elapsed since he'd entered the cargo hold he'd learned many things, the most significant of which was the threat posed by an angry monkey with a strong throwing arm and a good supply of poo.

"This is some sort of punishment for wanting to go via the City, right?"

"Not at all," the AllFather replies. "It's simply the logical result of a long unfamiliar journey. Really."

"What are you doing here?" asked Tallenna. "Who's supposed to be looking after you?"

"What's it to you?" said Kallie, suspiciously. "I don't need no-one to look after me!" She put her hands on her hips and looked the ornithopter up and down. "Are you going to pay me to look after your ship, or what?"

"I think I should look after you," whispered Tallenna to herself. She patted the girl on the arm. "You look half-starved. Why don't you come with me and I'll buy you some breakfast."

"Oh for pity's sake!" shouts the Warrior. "She's just flavour! Her, the Lord Mayor's rubbish tip, everything, it's all just fluff that he's made up in some kind of attempt to impress us. But it's all completely irrelevant to the actual thing we're supposed to be doing."

He slumps down in his chair, dispirited. "Just pay her the five silver crowns and then go do your talking to all your wizard friends so we can get out of here and actually get something done."

The AllFather looks from him to the Dealer and then back to him.

"Are either of you two doing anything?"

"I'm staying here!" declares the Warrior.

"I'll climb down and stretch my legs," says the Dealer.

"I'm climbing down too," says the Warrior.

Kallie watched as two more figures climbed down from the glass house mounted atop the strange craft. The first figure was unusual, but not unfamiliar – a painted barbarian of the type who occasionally came to the City, grunting with excitement at shop window displays, and leaving the public privvies in states that had citizens shaking their heads and aspiring politicians calling for legislation.

The second was very familiar, terrifyingly so, for if Kallie had not seen him before – and how could she know, with his face half hidden behind an open helm? – she had seen the type. She had seen men clad in that night-black armour. Had seen what they did. Knew what they were.

As he dropped to the ground to stand beside the barbarian she raised her arm and shouted at the top of her lungs.

"It's a child-snatcher!"

"Something you want to tell us?" asks the Jester, looking at the Warrior with eyebrows raised and the trace of a mocking smile on his lips.

"She has mistaken me for someone else!"

"Someone who also wears black armour?" suggests the Lady, no humour in her voice.

"I do not know. But I have never... snatched children!"

"Well there was that orphanage," the Dealer points out.

"I did not kidnap any of its children!" snaps the Warrior.

"No!" says the Jester, laughing. "You left them all locked inside when you burned it down!"

"I needed a sacrifice to power a spell," the Warrior mutters unhappily. "I am a paladin of darkness!"

"Exactly," shouts the AllFather. "You serve an evil cause and an evil god and are allied to evil people. So you can't complain when you have to face the consequences of that evil."

"But this is not fair!" protests the Warrior. "Draag is honourable evil. You're making him look sordid, somehow like a.."

He searches for a word.

The Jester supplies one. "Nonce!" he says, ignoring the Warrior's resulting glare.

"Draag is evil!" says the AllFather. "Not good evil, not honourable evil, just evil. It's more than just cool-looking black armour and necromantic spells you know!"

"Fine!" the Warrior declares. "You want me to be evil and he doesn't want to pay the five silver crowns and she wants us all to waste time in this dump. Well never let it be said that I don't try to advance the storyline."

Draag knelt down in front of the little girl and smiled what he'd been assured by experts was a trust-inducing smile.

"Hello little girl. My name's Draag. If you can help me with a little task I've got I'll give you ten silver crowns!"

"This is beyond all that is decent and acceptable and I'm having nothing to do with it!" the Lady tells the AllFather.

The Jester grimaces. "I'm feeling a bit queasy myself."

"Do not blame me," says the Warrior. "I'm only playing my character as directed. It was not I who introduced the concept of child sacrifice into the game, was it?"

The AllFather shifts awkwardly. "Well I don't think we need to play through everything that happens in great detail. Perhaps it would help if you each described what you wanted to do in this visit."

"Well I might as well head off and purchase some useful supplies," says the Dealer.

Yann shifted his backpack until the straps rested comfortably across his shoulders and its back rested neatly against his spine, and then set out, saying: "I'm off to buy supplies."

"I'll head off to the nearest temple of my order to make an appropriate sacrifice."

"Sacrifice?" asked the Lady, raising a suspicious eyebrow.

"Don't worry," the Warrior tells her. "I'll pick up another street kid along the way."

Many times the AllFather has regretted allowing the Warrior to create an evil mortal, but never more so than now. Though his eyes are firmly fixed on the tablets before him, he can still sense the Lady's cold-eyed glare boring into the side of his head.

"I perhaps should point out that Tallenna is unaware of what Draag plans to do," he tells her, his eyes still firmly locked on the tablets.

"I envy her," he hears her mutter.

Kallie watched as the black-clad paladin picked his way through the festering mounds of rubbish.

"I don't like him!" she said.

"No-one likes him," said the woman, shaking her head before squatting down in front of Kallie again. She looked kind and gentle. Hardened and suspicious and streetwise as she was, something inside Kallie said she should trust her.

The woman took Kallie's hands in hers.

"I'm going to take you somewhere where there are people who will feed you, protect you, love you, and teach you."

"I suddenly feel an overwhelming urge to vomit!" the Warrior declares, jabbing his finger towards his mouth in an exaggerated mime.

"Welcome to our world," the Jester tells him, looking slightly ill. Beside him, the Dealer nods, an equally pained expression.

The AllFather coughs. "And what did you want to do, Lord Jester?"

"Oh yeah. I've got some stuff."

"Stuff?"

Jansen watched the human sorceress walk away, hand-in-hand with the young girl who'd offered to watch the ship. He didn't quite understand what had just happened, and suspected he never would.

He looked around at the spot where he'd landed. Pile upon pile of refuse sat festering beneath a smoke-filled sky. This was a terrible place, and one that both scared and disturbed him.

His thoughts were interrupted by the sights and sounds of the miniature humanoid trying, and failing, to attach a saddle and saddlebags to a dog that currently was refusing to stand.

A rapid burst of speech then erupted from the halfling, a burst that Jansen did not entirely manage to follow. However, he was reasonably confident that he'd managed to grasp the essential themes of the resulting "conversation" which were, in no particular order, unhappiness, betrayal, loyalty and recriminations – with recriminations apparently being a recurring theme on both sides of the conversation, whether communicated by speech, hand-waving, whining, or ground-pawing.

Eventually, negotiations appeared to be concluded and the dog stood up. The small humanoid finished cinching the various leather straps, climbed up onto the saddle, and then rode off without a word.

Jansen walked a slow circuit around his ship, kicking at a few items of rubble, and feeling very, very alone. Then he remembered that one of his passengers still remained aboard the ship, the unspeaking warrior with the rusty armour and the vacant eyes. He looked up: the warrior still sat in the cockpit, staring ahead as though unaware that they'd landed. Jansen shook his head.

This was a strange place.

Home to a strange people.

Draag's religion was not a hypocritical one. While followers of other faiths preached modesty and humility, but then built temples that reached for the sky and shone like the sun, the City's Cathedral of Darkness was built entirely underground, its only public face a discrete black door in an undistinguished back alley.

Draag knocked on the door. Once, twice, once, and once again.

A moment later a small sliding panel set into the door slid aside, revealing only darkness.

"Yes!" snapped an unseen voice.

"It is I, Draag. I have returned and wish to make worship before the forces of darkness."

The door opened to reveal a small chamber, dimly lit by flicking oil lamps. Inside was a figure clad in a dark, hooded robe, his face hidden by shadow. "Enter, Brother Draag," he said. "Welcome home."

He reached into an alcove and pulled out a black robe identical to the one he wore. "Put on the sacred robes brother, and proceed to the chamber. The priests of darkness are waiting."

A tapping on his armour clad leg roused Draag from his thoughts.

"Yes?" he snapped.

A small piercing voice came from below. "When do I get my five crowns?"

"Anyway," says the AllFather. "I think we can leave that there. You gain five points of spiritual renewal and then make your way back to the ornithopter."

"That's is not fair," protests the Warrior. "I am being deprived of the possibility of a roleplaying bonus!"

He thumps the table.

"You should not have allowed me to create an evil mortal if you were not prepared to allow me to guide him as you yourself stipulated!"

"He's got a point," says the Jester. "You're the one who came up with the whole child-snatcher thing."

For some time now an unwelcome feeling of sickness has been squatting in the pit of the AllFather's stomach like a stray dog found sleeping in front of a fire, who merely growls when leaving is suggested.

Every now and again such dogs stand up, shake themselves, and walk round in a circle treading down the fireside rug before dropping back down to sleep.

Right now, the AllFather feels like the sick feeling in his stomach is circling and treading and flopping back down. He can't remember why he thought it would be a good idea to illustrate the depths of Draag's evil by introducing the idea of child sacrifice. Hindsight has shown it to be a terrible idea, but he suspects that foresight could have performed the task equally well.

He sighs.

Four pairs of eyes glare at him, all displaying various levels of anger.

He needs to take charge.

He is the god of gods.

He is he who turned nothing to dust and dust to a universe.

He is he who is master of all.

He sighs again.

"You can have seven points then."

Chapter Eleven

The OverRealm; what would again be some time later if the AllFather had ever got around to installing time.

The room is silent save for a rhythmic tapping. It is annoying, but apparently not annoying enough, for no-one has yet commented on it even though it has been going on for some considerable amount of what ends up passing for time here.

"In the name of everything!" explodes the Warrior, finally. "Am I just supposed to sit here while these three stumble through their tedious subplots?" He points at the Dealer, who is currently making notes on a slate, brow creased in concentration as he performs some mental arithmetic. "Between him haggling at the market, her–" he points at the Lady "–attempting to coach a pre-teen gangster through the Institute's entry exams, and him–" he points at the Jester "–going around... what exactly are you doing?"

The Jester shrugs. "Like I said. I've got some stuff."

The City was not home territory for Hill's people, but enough of them had found their way there that the sight of one of "the people" riding a dog through its streets did not provoke any strange glances.

Indeed, he had already passed several of his compatriots, and with each had exchanged what halflings referred to as "the wave", that apparently casual gesture that conveyed greetings, promised assistance, and suggested a willingness to engage in business dealings that other less enlightened races might term theft.

So far though, they'd all just waved back.

He'd also worn his chalk so low scratching street-runes on street-corners that he swore the last two or three had been fifty percent chalk and fifty percent blood and mashed flesh.

But when he'd ridden a second circuit past his freshly chalked signs, he'd seen no chalked replies.

Things were getting desperate. It seemed like the universe was conspiring to teach him a very unwelcome truth.

He was going to have to pay a visit to Big Rick.

The Jester is not happy. This is perhaps a redundant statement, since none of those sitting around the table could currently be described as happy with the possible exception of the Sleeper, who could more accurately be described as either bored or confused – or quite possibly both.

But as it is the Jester who is currently the focus of the AllFather's attention, it is he who could be described as more actively unhappy.

"So let me get this straight," he says. "The entire membership of all three Thieves' Guilds have apparently gone straight?"

"No," says the AllFather carefully. "They just aren't responding to your invitations. You don't know why."

"I've got a rough idea," says the Jester bitterly. "You've been planning this ever since I said Hill was going to steal some of the elves' stuff, haven't you?"

Like a faithfully regular geyser, the Warrior explodes once more. "That's it! If you're going to make him spend the next three days trying to fence the elves' stuff, then I'm off. Let me know when you're ready for us to actually do something!"

He strides out, slamming the door behind him, and as a result only half-hears the AllFather's quiet, muttered response.

"They're not elves."

Ogres, as a race, are not prone to attacks of either subtlety or humour, which is why Big Rick was not, as most would assume, small for an ogre, but was in fact a giant.

Ogres, as a race, are also not prone to value intellect over brawn, something illustrated by the fact that when the elected leader of the City's ogre community stood to greet Hill, he bashed his head into his office's ceiling.

"Ouch!" he shouted. He sat down, rubbing his head with a pained expression on his face, then added. "Sorry. Gets me every time. Built for humans, you know?"

"Not really," said Hill, climbing into a chair two sizes too big for him.

Big Rick clasped his hands together and leaned forward, his brow furrowed in concentration as his mouth opened but words failed to come out.

"What can you do for me?" suggested Hill.

The ogre nodded enthusiastically for a second until the couple of randomly firing brain neurons tasked with calculating the next line in the conversation fired in a way that was both random and wrong. Confusion returned to his flat and creased face. "I don't know," he whispered. "What can I do for you?"

We have already established that time is something that the AllFather has never quite got around to installing in the OverRealm.

Unfortunately, the situation with space isn't much better, with the result that the total interior space of the OverRealm lies somewhere between "from the ends of eternity to the far side of infinity" and "imagine a reasonably sized country house" depending on just quite what you mean by the word "space".

Given that the OverRealm is, as has already been mentioned, home to not only the Gods – of which there is a depressingly large and inefficient number – but several thousand assorted minions also, this lack of an answer to the question "just how big is this place, anyway?" is something that the Warrior has complained about several times over the aeons.

The Warrior is quite willing to do something about it himself; whilst what pass for the OverRealm's laws of reality are the responsibility of the AllFather, eliminating the overpopulation problem by eliminating the population would, he feels, be right up his street. In fact, in the distressingly vague period of non-time since he left the table, the Warrior has already reduced the OverRealm's minion population from several thousand to several thousand less two.

Of course, this is only a temporary state of affairs, and the two eliminated minions will eventually arrive back at the OverRealm clutching much-stamped temporal passports, telling tales of a brief but eventful tour of each of the twelve and a half planes of existence, and complaining of the fate of their baggage, which will no doubt still be stuck somewhere in the sixth or seventh plane.

As with most things, this is – in the opinion of the Warrior – entirely the fault of the AllFather, given that it is entirely due to a severe design constraint in the design of the universe in which souls cannot be destroyed but instead can only be shuffled from place to place.

This has three main effects.

Firstly, minions – having made it into the OverRealm's afterlife – have a job not simply for life, but for all eternity, the result of that knowledge being a catastrophic drop in productivity.

Secondly, the totals all have to add up or the Accountant, Lord of Man's Obsessiveness, will spend a sleepless non-night trying to account for the missing souls in his double entry balance sheet.

Thirdly... thirdly is something that the Warrior has not yet worked out – but since it is a basic rule of both universes and narratives that things come in threes, the Warrior is pretty sure there will be one, sooner or later.

In the meantime, annoying the hell out of the Lord of Man's Obsessiveness will do for the moment.

The Warrior crooks his finger at a minion attempting to slide past him on the opposite side of the passage.

"Oy you!" he shouts. "Come over here."

"I've got some stuff," said Hill.

"Stuff?" queried Big Rick.

"Yes," agreed Hill. "Stuff."

"Right. Okay. Stuff is good."

Hill agreed that stuff was indeed good and then they sat looking at each other as wave after wave of confusion arrived upon Big Rick's face and set up camp.

"Would you like to see the stuff?" said Hill, when he couldn't bear it any more.

"Stuff?" asked Big Rick.

"So he's an amnesiac as well as stupid, is he?" asks the Jester.
"Ogres have an entirely different way of thinking," says the AllFather. "I don't think it's appropriate to describe them as either stupid or amnesiac."
"Fine. I'll show him the stuff then, shall I?"

Big Rick examined the Wesh artefacts one by one. "Shiny," he pronounced solemnly.

"Shiny," agreed Hill.

The ogre picked up the shiniest of the artefacts, a silver ball, and gave it an experimental shake. Nothing happened, so he gave it another shake, at which point anything at all again failed to happen.

Hill reached forward, carefully tugged it from his grasp, and pressed the hidden stud on its base that had – to be fair – required a good deal of poking and prodding for him to find when he'd first acquired it.

The effect was instantaneous: centred on the silver ball's equator, and extending for perhaps a foot and a half in either direction, was a perfect miniature landscape. It was much like the display the Priest of Priests had shown them, except that this one showed a fixed pastoral view which wobbled sickeningly until Hill placed the ball back onto the table.

"Ooh..." said Big Rick, entranced. "Ahh..." He moved his finger around the projected image, stopping on each feature.

"Tree!"

"Yes," said Hill. "Tree."

"Dogs!"

"Yes," said Hill. "Dogs."

"Sheeps!"

It was at this moment, as frustration was morphing gracefully into tedium, that the girl walked into the room. She was beautiful, and slim, and when Hill stood up to greet her he found himself looking down into the bluest eyes he'd ever seen.

"Hang on a minute..."
"What?" asks the AllFather, suspicious.
"You said I was looking down into her eyes?"
"You are. She's a pixie. She's two foot nine. Why?"
"That's tall enough for me."

Hill let his lips linger just a moment on her hand as he kissed it, then stood up straight to gaze into her eyes and give her the smile that would make her his.

"Hey baby," he told her. "What sort of name does a beautiful girl like you have?"

"But she's a pixie!" stutters the AllFather, flustered.
  "And?"
  "And you're not!"
  "Doesn't bother me," says the Jester, shrugging. "I'm not prejudiced."
  "Well she is!"
  "She might not like big feet," suggests the Dealer.
  "Or she might just have taste," suggests the Lady.
  The AllFather taps the table for silence. Romance makes him nervous at the best of times. "Hill is your mortal, but I should warn you that for a cross-species seduction to work you'll need a lot of successes, and failure is liable to result in a great deal of bad feeling."
  "How many successes?"
  The AllFather thinks for a moment. "Five."
  The knuckle-bones bounce across the table.
  "Will seven do?"

Hill sat back down on the chair, pulling the girl back down with him so that she ended up sitting on his lap. For a moment she looked shocked, angry even. But then something inside her visibly melted, and she relaxed into his embrace, smiling.

"My name's Shenna," she said.

"Well good day to you Shenna!" said Hill brightly. "My name's Hill." He looked across the table at the confused figure of Big Rick. "Rick mate," he told him. "You got anything nice to drink round here?"

"Er... Well there's some wine out back."

Hill had by this time turned his attention back to Shenna, so he just waved a hand in the ogre's direction as he spoke. "Cool, that'll do. Be a diamond and bring it though with a couple of glasses, yeah?"

"Er..."

"Oh, and have you got any biscuits?"

The AllFather took a deep breath. "You really think he's going to allow you to treat him like that, in his own office?"
  "Hey, I've got charm," says the Jester.
  "You'll need a bucket-load."
  "How much?"
  "Nine successes."
  The knuckle-bones dance across the table. Tappity, tappity, tappity. Silence. Then an awed sigh and a muttered "What a fluke..." from the Dealer.

not actually need to eat they nonetheless do, for exactly the same reasons that mortals will reach for a second helping of chicken or a first helping of kebab.

It's something to pass the time with.

The Warrior is not searching for any particular kind of food; instead, he is searching for anything but a particular kind of food.

Anything other than ambrosia, to be precise.

Ambrosia might be the food of the gods, but the Warrior has always considered it to be a rather tasteless gloop entirely unsuitable for one such as himself.

Alas, since the kitchen staff are no more hard-working than the rest of the OverRealm's minions, the menu for lunch usually consists of a starter of ambrosia followed by ambrosia with ambrosia for desert.

This is not a fact that the AllFather is unaware of; the Warrior can be sure of that because he himself has complained more times than there are grains of sands in the southern deserts.

Well a lot, anyhow.

It is the Warrior's considered opinion that the AllFather has only two techniques for dealing with a problem for which he alone is responsible: either a pitiful, hand-wringing assertion that there is nothing he can do; or a bungled attempt to fix the problem that, in an effort to avoid creating upset, totally avoids the actual cause.

The Warrior now stands before one of the results of the AllFather's desire to avoid all interpersonal conflict.

He looks over the brightly coloured pictures that adorn the metal box's front and settles upon one which looks something like the dish that mortals term steak.

Beneath the picture is a square red button.

He presses it.

Hill counted out the last wad of money and, satisfied that all was correct and proper, placed it on top of the pile that had, over the last five minutes, taken over a good chunk of Big Rick's desk.

"Sixty thousand crowns,"

The desk's owner hovered, slightly hunched, by the door, unsure about exactly what was happening.

"So that's sixty thousand... for the stuff?" he asked.

"That's the deal," Hill told him brightly. "And a very good one it is too." He strode over to the ogre and held up his hand.

"Good doing business with you!"

The ogre shook, the confused expression on his face apparently settling in for a lengthy stay.

Hill turned to the girl, and reached out for her hands.

"Shenna?"

Her eyes looked up at him, excitement and anticipation sparkling in the

blueness. "Yes Hill?" she breathed.
   "It was good doing business with you too."

Chapter Thirteen

The OverRealm. Several not-seconds have now elapsed since the AllFather's announcement of the theft of the final ring.

The Warrior is standing, his chair pushed angrily back. To say that he is not pleased with this turn of events would be to understate things by an extreme amount, the degree of which can be demonstrated by one salient fact.

The Jester has not yet laughed.

Those robed figures still sitting at the table exchange uneasy glances, but say nothing.

Twelve legs and ten eyeballs stood and watched as the monkey scampered across the sand with the ring clutched in one paw. It headed up the steep face of the dune opposite and disappeared over the crest, with only footprints left behind.

Silence settled upon the desert, broken only by the faint whistle of wind across the sand.

The Warrior sits back down. "I will attack the monkey! It shall not be allowed to steal what is mine!"

The AllFather pauses, perturbed over a minor, but sentence stopping issue, which is how to refer to the "monkey". Because while the "monkey" is not, in fact, a monkey, but is instead a member of an intelligent sentient race, this is a piece of information which none of the gods have ever got round to obtaining.

"I said I'm going to attack the monkey!"

The AllFather sighs a private mental sigh. "I did say that the monkey was running up the far face of the dune and you chose to do nothing."

"I did not choose to do nothing! I was thinking!"

"Fine. And so was Draag."

"That is not correct. Just because I am thinking does not mean that Draag is thinking. I think! Draag reacts!"

The Lady smiles. "Is that because he's cleverer than you?"

"He is not cleverer than me!"

"Legendaryintellect!" coughs the Jester.

"My own intellect is at least legendary!" says the Warrior, ignoring the Jester's raised eyebrow. "Perhaps even epic." He picks up his knuckle-bones. "As soon as the monkey attempted to steal the ring, Draag would have reacted to stop him!"

He casts the knuckle-bones across the table.

"Three successes!" he announces. "I have grappled the monkey before it gets hold of the ring."

The Dealer taps him on the arm. "In this heat you have to make a resistance test before any action, and you have been wearing full

99

armour..."

"...for several hours," adds the Lady. "And you haven't been drinking much water either, so you'd need at least, what?"

"Five successes," says the Jester. "And that's not including the fact that his armour's metal, so it will now be hot enough to fry eggs on. I'd say that makes six."

The Lady smiles at the Warrior. "Still, it's good to have you back with us!"

It all happened very quickly. As Hill pushed the ring onto the monkey's finger and it drank, the gleam in its eyes returned, and its other paw reached out to snatch the one remaining ring.

Seeing this, Draag let out an enraged cry, reached out an arm, and toppled unconscious to the ground like a falling log. The monkey dodged out from underneath him and set off up the far dune with the ring clutched in its paw.

Hill watched, then turned his attention back to Draag, who was lying face down in the sand.

"Do you reckon he's dead then?"

"Look I make the decisions round here!" snaps the AllFather.

"Are you sure?" asks the Jester.

"Yes!"

"So what's the decision then?"

Yann looked at the apparently lifeless body of the fallen dark paladin. "Might be."

Hill gave the body a poke with his foot. "He might just have fainted."

A bead of sweat appears on the AllFather's brow. "Perhaps we should just summarise the situation?" he suggests.

The Jester smiles. "Certainly. Lord Warrior went on strike, which you ignored. He then decided to end the strike when the monkey stole his ring, at which point we pointed out that since he was several casts of the knuckle-bones overdue, his first cast upon resuming the game would count as the first of those overdue casts, and since his knuckle-bones did not smile upon him in that cast, his mortal is now lying face down in the desert attempting to breathe through sand." He looks around the table. "Is that a fair summary?"

The AllFather glares at him, hurt. "I was actually suggesting that I might summarise the situation."

"Oh you were stalling," says the Jester, oozing fake sincerity. "I'm sorry, I didn't know."

The Warrior bangs the table. "Your summary is not correct! My mortal is not lying face down in the sand!"

Draag pushed hard up the dune, stopped, and aimed DeathSinger's blade at

estimated didn't match that which his inner senses told him it should be.
Either the sun had moved from its prescribed track.
Or the land beneath him had shifted.
He called down to Hill. "I think the rock face is moving upward!"
The answer came back thin and distorted. "What?"
"The rock face. I think it's moving upward!"

The Jester peers at the knuckle-bones sitting before him. "One success?"

"You've got a baroque face with too much wood?" shouted Hill, hanging back in his harness, his arms outstretched in confusion.

"Hang on," shouted Yann. "I'll come down." He quickly rappelled down, easing to a halt just beside the halfling. He gathered his breath for a moment, and then spoke. "The rock face. It's moving upward."

"What? The whole thing?"

"Yes. All the features around us are in the same place relative to each other. But they've all moved relative to the sun."

"By how much?"

"Forty, maybe fifty miles."

"But if the entire rock face is lifting, then that means... that means the entire head is lifting!"

"Exactly. The question is, why?"

"The land has definitely shifted up?" says the Dealer.
The AllFather nods. "Definitely."
"But couldn't it just be the side-to-side rocking of the world serpent? The motion that produces the tides?"
"No. This is in addition to that movement."
The Dealer and the Jester trade confused glances.

Hill looked sideways, to where the giant unblinking eye observed half a universe, and downward, towards the black shadow that marked a nostril fully fifty miles across. A vision came to him, of tiny dots moving across a giant snout.

"I've got a horrible feeling I know what's about to happen."

"And what's that?"

"I think this thing's about to sneeze."

107

Chapter Fifteen

Silence has settled around the table, save for the slurping of the Warrior as he finishes the last of his ambrosia.

"Look, I get that," says the Jester. "I get that the whole sneeze thing is your way of telling us that we're not supposed to spend a year abseiling down the rock face to go with the year we spent walking here."

"I can't comment," says the AllFather. "But that is a reasonable conclusion to draw."

"Fine. But what I don't get... hang on a minute, does that mean we didn't need to spend a year walking here either?"

The AllFather smiles and shrugs.

"Whatever. We get that there's a quicker way of doing it. What we don't get is what that quicker way is." He looks around at his fellow gods. "Is that a reasonable summary?"

They nod.

The AllFather spreads his arms apologetically. "It's your problem, for your mortals to solve."

The Warrior swears under his breath. "Damned problem solving. When do we get some combat?"

Day nine, early morning. Draag eased the control rope in and kicked hard against the rock, sending him swooping downward in a series of lazy bounces. A couple of hundred feet later he dropped to a halt on a narrow ledge beside Hill.

"Oh it's you," said the halfling.

Draag knew Hill hated him, but he didn't care. The halfling was chaotic and unreliable in nature, rude and disrespectful in personality, and a thief. (He was still particularly upset about the dried banana chips).

"It is. Were you expecting someone else?"

"One can always hope."

Draag didn't answer, but instead began the process of disengaging himself from the main rope, waiting for another snappy put-down from the halfling. When that didn't come he looked up, and saw Hill staring intently into the sky.

"What is it?"

"Over there, see?"

Draag followed Hill's outstretched hand, but saw nothing save clear blue sky.

"You are blind and a fool. I see nothing."

"Well I do, which makes you blind for not seeing it, and a fool for disregarding me."

"There is nothing there!" declared Draag, looking again at the sky – and seeing a series of specks heading towards them.

"This is not fair!" says the Warrior.
"How is it not fair?" asks the AllFather.
"I cast more successes than he to look at the sky and was told by you that I could see nothing."
"And I told Lord Jester that he could see something."
"But I had more successes, so my mortal should have been right and his wrong!"
The Jester coughs. "Lord Warrior. My mortal has better sight than yours. So it was my mortal who was right and yours who was wrong."
"But I have spectacles of eagle's sight!"
"So have I."
"But you're not wearing any spectacles!"
"Contacts."

Hill looked up the rock face; Yann was a hundred or so feet above and descending, the others mere ants beyond him. Hill pointed at the rapidly approaching specks and shouted.

"Incoming!"

Yann looked out for a moment, then looked down, giving a thumbs up of confirmation, before turning to look up the rock face, and shouting.

The Sleeper peers across the table. "One... two... three successes?"
The AllFather speaks. "Yann's voice is thin and distorted, but you can clearly make out the word, incoming."
"Okay."
Five faces stare at him, but he somehow fails to notice. The stares eventually turn to smiles and resigned shrugs, but he manages to not notice those too.
"Contacts!" snorts the Warrior. "I've never heard anything so ridiculous in all of eternity."
"Says the man who's wearing eleven rings."
"At least my rings are genre appropriate."
"Lord Pervert might agree with you. I doubt anyone else would."
Silence settles. The Dealer smiles an encouraging, hinting smile at the Sleeper and the Sleeper smiles back. The Dealer shoulder flinches a suggestion at the AllFather and the AllFather smiles knowingly and infuriatingly back.
"Where's Shovel?" asks the Jester.
"Just a little way above Stone," says the AllFather. "Tallenna was winding him, the monkey, and the backpacks down."
"Okay, for the monkey..."
The knuckle-bones dance.
"...and for the dog."

109

They dance again.

The AllFather mentally calculates for a moment, then looks at the Lady. "Mistress Lady?"

She tosses her knuckle-bones across the table. "Three successes?"

"You can hear a noise from below. It's Shovel barking. Looking down you can see that the monkey is prodding the dog with one hand and pointing out to the sky with the other."

"Well it's nice that someone cares enough about me to let me know," says the Lady, looking pointedly at the Sleeper.

He blinks. "Know what? Sorry, was I supposed to tell you something?"

Yann bounced down onto the ledge and disconnected himself from the rope. The specks were arcing in fast, too fast. He muttered an angry curse. He wasn't particularly counting on the wind spirits of the northern plains sending a tornado either quite this far south nor quite this far off the edge of the world – but it was both satisfying and comforting to call for one anyway.

And spread out like this – himself, Draag and Hill on the ledge, Stone and the animals perhaps three hundred feet above them, and Tallenna perhaps three hundred feet more – they'd need all the help they could get.

But recriminations were for later, if there was a later. Survival was all that mattered now, and while he, Draag and Hill fought together here, those above them would have to fight their own lonely battles.

He pulled his long bow off his back and pulled an arrow from his quiver.

Closer.

Closer.

"Now look!" shouts the AllFather. "Everything's happening very quickly, and I'm not going to let you do your normal trick of bringing the entire game to a grinding halt while you discuss every possible strategy. You can do one thing and one thing only. Now one at a time."

"I will unsheathe DeathSinger, aim it at the approaching objects, and back into the rock face in a crouching position," says the Warrior.

"That's three," says the Jester, holding up three fingers. "Unless you include crouching down, in which case it's four."

"That is not so."

"Well let's call it three and a half then."

"Enough!" snaps the AllFather. "That counts as one thing, and I'd appreciate it if you'd confine your comments to telling me what you intend your mortal to do."

"I'll take my crossbow out, load a magazine in, and give the clockwork a good few winds."

"Now that's three actions!" shouts the Warrior.

The AllFather nods. "I'll let you get away with loading the magazine, but the clockwork action takes several seconds to fully wind."

"This is not fair," says the Jester, in an exaggerated and mimicked voice.

"Are you mocking me?"

"Not at all," the Jester says to the Warrior. "Why would you think I am?"

The Warrior glares at him for a few seconds, then speaks. "That weapon is completely inappropriate, anyway. Clockwork is for novelty toys and timepieces and has no place on the battlefield!"

The Dealer waves a finger in agreement. "I am forced to agree with Lord Warrior. I'm not at all convinced that such a weapon should be feasible. I do not think that it complies with reasonable laws of reality."

The Jester points at the AllFather. "He cleared it."

"Mistress Lady?" says the AllFather quickly.

"I'll cast Spider's Cradle on myself to anchor myself to the rock-face."

"Good. And Lord Sleeper?"

The Sleeper points at the Warrior. "I'll do what he's doing."

"He's drawing his sword and crouching down on the rock ledge."

"I'll do that."

"You can't. You're not on the ledge."

"Aren't I?"

"No, you're not. You're hanging in a harness off the rope about three hundred feet above the ledge. That's why Lord Dealer was having to shout up to you."

"Oh. I thought I would have climbed down by now? I did say Stone was climbing down."

"You did. But only a few seconds have passed by since then."

"Oh right. Seems longer."

"Yes. Yes it does. So what do you want to do?"

"Get out my sword?"

"Well if that's what you want to do."

"Have I finished winding the clockwork yet?"

"Oh alright, yes."

"That is not fair!"

Hill gave the loading crank a final turn and snapped the crossbow up to his shoulder. The approaching objects showed crystal clear and terrifyingly large in the crossbow's telescopic sight; balls of what looked like molten tar that flamed and crackled and left a burning trail of–

"And I think that telescopic sight's highly suspect, also," says the Dealer.

"Hey, I did some deals for a couple of gnomes who used to work the docks. They knew people, you know?"

"I'm trying to give you a description here!" snaps the AllFather.

"Sorry, carry on. Flavour's good."

The AllFather glares at him for a moment and then continues speaking.

-sparks as they swooped through the air. Hill rested his cheek against the crossbow's polished rosewood stock and breathed slowly.

In.

Out.

In.

Out.

Closer.

Closer.

Closer.

"Now!" shouted Yann.

Hill gave the trigger a momentary squeeze and a bolt shot away, followed an instant later by a second and then a third, the clockwork screaming as it rammed bolts into the chamber and pulled the drawstring back, the butt thudding reassuringly into his shoulder.

Through the scope he saw his bolts ram home, tearing, cutting and finally smashing through in an explosion of tar and fire.

He shifted aim, found a second target, and fired another three bolt burst. The bolts - off-centre - hit only glancing blows, and the thing flew on, leaving a trail of incandescent blobs of something in its wake.

He moved, tracked, prepared to fire - and saw it explode as a long arrow punched through its centre and blew it into fragments.

Yann.

A quick high five and they were back in action, Yann's arrows taking out two of the incoming flame beasts while Hill dispatched three more before his magazine clicked empty.

He ducked back against the rock, ejected the spent magazine and pulled a fresh replacement from his belt pouch, simultaneously taking the chance to see what the world outside the scope was looking like.

The sky was full of flame-beasts, dozens of them, one hit as he watched by an arrow of Yann's, another disintegrated from above by a bolt of green lightning - Tallenna, he realised, covering them from her perch more than six hundred feet above. Beside him, Draag was firing jet after jet of flame from DeathSinger, but though each jet hit a flame-beast dead centre, it had no effect. The beasts simply flew through and out the other side.

"Give it up man!" Hill shouted. "It's got no effect on them." He slammed the fresh magazine into place and moved back into a firing crouch.

Draag screamed in frustration and anger; a continuous jet now streamed from the sword's point, filling the sky with flame. But still the beasts flew on, dipping, swooping, approaching.

"Leave it!"

"No!"

The world was back to just a small circle now. Hill breathed in, becoming one with the weapon, ignoring the flame that filled his view, searching, seeking – there!

Firing.

"This is not fair!"

The AllFather sighs. "How is it not fair?"

"You have constructed a scenario where my weapon is impotent!"

The Jester laughs. "Considering where you've placed that ring of protection, DeathSinger isn't the weapon I'd be worried about becoming impotent!"

He goes to speak again, but is silenced by the AllFather's glare.

"I have not constructed anything. These beasts live in an environment of perpetual and extreme heat. Not only that, they themselves incorporate flame as part of their bodies. Flame is to them what blood is to your mortals. Flame is not going to hurt them."

"That is a circular argument. You have constructed an environment whose inhabitants are likely to be immune to my primary weapon and then tell me that they are immune because of their environment."

"It is not a circular argument!" snaps the AllFather.

"Well it is a bit of one," says the Jester.

"Look, it's hot, they're flame, DeathSinger's useless! Okay! Can we please get back to the game?"

Yann had lost count of the number of beasts he'd dispatched from the skies; he knew only that his quiver, which had started the combat full, was noticeably lighter now.

Again and again the beasts dipped in, some so close that he felt their heat burning at his skin even through the protection of the Wesh's magic. But again and again the beasts fell, held at bay by either his arrows, or by the trusty figure of Hill, who stood beside him firing burst after burst, pausing only to slap fresh magazines into his crossbow.

"How many magazines have you got, anyhow?" asks the Dealer.

"As many as we need," the Jester replies. "It's a magical pouch."

The Lady leans forward with a quizzical expression on her face. "You have a pouch that magically produces metal magazines pre-filled with crossbow bolts?"

"Sure, what's the problem?"

"Well it's not exactly genre appropriate," says the Dealer.

The Jester shrugs. "The gnomes threw it in as part of the deal."

"This is not fair!"

Draag sat back against the rock, sulking, and thinking evil thoughts. With DeathSinger impotent against the flame beasts, he had little do do in the combat save sit and watch as the halfling and the barbarian fired shot after shot at the attacking waves.

He could have offered his encouragement, but quite frankly, that was not his way.

He found a small pebble lying on the ledge beside him, and picked it up, twirling it around between his gauntleted fingers and imagining it was the halfling's neck.

It felt good.

Especially when he squeezed.

After a few minutes he sensed a slackening of fire from his two companions, and looked up. The flame-beasts were withdrawing – or perhaps regrouping?

The beasts formed up, swooped away, and climbed.

"They're going for Stone and the equipment!" shouted the barbarian.

"My bloody animals are up there!" shouted the halfling.

The halfling hung his crossbow across his back and set off up the rope, not bothering to use his metal spiders but instead simply hauling himself up hand over hand.

The barbarian looked down at Draag.

"You coming?"

"It is not my fight. And besides, I have been rendered useless by their immunity to fire."

"I think he's back on strike," mutters the Lady.

"So what are you actually going to do?" asks the AllFather.

"I shall stay where I am and observe."

"You're not actually going to do anything?"

"I shall practice my sword strokes."

The creatures were cold. It sensed that. And it hated the cold. Wanted, needed, was compelled to extinguish the cold.

When they had first come upon the cold things they had struck out, without thought or plan. And the cold things had punished them for it, firing cold rods of death that had sent scores of its packmates to the seas of heaven below.

All things eventually lost their grip on life, reached that day when they could no longer maintain altitude, and began their fall to the afterlife. But that was a slow, dignified fall that formed part of the cycle of life – not this violent slaying of those who were young and who still soared high and proud this far up the wall of the world.

Now they hated the cold things, wanted revenge, and would strive to achieve it. There were more cold things, higher up the wall; weaker perhaps? It arced, turned, and followed its packmates into the attack.

The AllFather turns his attention to the Sleeper. "What do you want to do?" he asks him.

"What's happening?"

The AllFather sighs. "Three of the flame-beasts are heading straight for you with two more heading for the harness containing the dog and the monkey."

"I'll try and parry them with my sword."

"Okay."

The Lady leans forward and touches the AllFather on the arm. "I'll cast two bolts of Green Lightning down, one at the first of the group heading for Stone, and one at the first of the group heading for the animals. And then I'll start readying a couple more."

"Am I there yet?" says the Jester.

"No. You're about two-thirds of the way up with the Dealer a little way behind you. I'll tell you when you get there."

"I'm climbing really fast!"

"I know."

When his new clan had started their descent of the biggest, widest tree Takes had ever seen, he'd been happy. He knew trees. Trees were good. Trees were where the people of the Folk sat in branches laughing at the beasts of the forest that couldn't climb.

Granted, sometimes it turned out that the beasts of the forest could climb (personally, Takes was of the opinion that using claws to climb rather than hands was cheating of the lowest order, but neither panthers nor bears seemed to give a damn) and then it wasn't always so funny – at least not until you worked out who was last in the queue for the upper branches and made sure it wasn't you.

Takes had stayed reasonably happy for the first few days of the climb, despite the big people's insistence on strapping him into some kind of web and attaching him to one of their vines. This was an insult, for after all, was he not the nimblest of the Folk?

And he wasn't particularly happy that, as always, they paired him with the thing with four legs and no hands that the little-but-still-big-person-who-fed-him-banana-chips called Shovel.

He never had managed to understand just what they thought he had in common with it. The thing was stupid, clumsy, and the worst conversationalist Takes had ever met.

And it smelt, too.

But as day followed day, and Takes started to realise just how big this tree was, he'd started to appreciate being dropped down in the big people's web.

Happiness was not a sign he would have used had anyone bothered to ask him how he was. But he wasn't quite not happy either.

Until the flame-things arrived.

No creature of the forest likes flame. But flame that flies and swoops and heads straight for you – that's another level of not liking altogether.

It was time to go mobile.

The Folk communicated using gestures, and Takes took a brief moment to send a couple of signed words at the four-legged thing, signs which broadly translated to: "So long sucker, I'm outta here!"

He knew the thing wouldn't understand, but he didn't see why that should deprive him of the final word. Then he quickly unsnapped the various catches that held him in the harness and headed on up the rope.

He wasn't quite sure where the rope headed, but it had to be better than here.

The AllFather scratches a few tally counts on his tablet and then looks up, trying to work out who he should speak to first.

His gaze settles upon the Lady.

"Right... Mistress Lady. You send down a couple of Green Lightning bolts and both strike home, sending two more of the flame-beasts spiralling down towards the sea that boils far, far below. And the monkey has now reached you. It tugs on your sleeve and gestures frantically."

"Good. How are Lord Dealer and Lord Jester doing down below? I'm thinking that perhaps I should send down some sort of fog?" She looks across the table at them. "That way you might be able to slip away."

"Risky," says the Dealer. "They might still be able to sense us, but we certainly won't be able to see them."

"Oh, and I'll give the monkey a quick stroke to calm its nerves."

"It gestures a lot more," says the AllFather. "Would you like to do a sense meaning test?"

She picks up the knuckle-bones, but then pauses. "Why?"

The Jester leans forward. "Are you saying it's intelligent, or something?"

"I'm not saying anything," replies the AllFather. "I'm just asking her to make the test."

The Lady shrugs, then tosses the knuckle-bones across the table. "Two successes."

"You think it is trying to tell you that heading up would be a good idea. Lord Jester?"

116

"Have I got to the dog yet?"

"Yes. You're next to him, with Lord Sleeper just a little way to the other side of you. In the distance you can just barely see a whole flight of flame-beasts heading in."

The Jester curses. "Have they not run out of bodies yet?"

"They must have bought up reinforcements," says the Dealer.

"Why? What did we do to them? Okay, well I'll set up a firing position here and shoot any flame-beasts that come my way."

"Good. You anchor yourself to a convenient crack and bring your crossbow into a firing position. Lord Dealer?"

"Is his firing position any better than the one I'm currently in?"

"Not noticeably so, I'm afraid."

"Then I'll stay where I am."

"Lord Warrior?"

"I will continue to practice my sword strokes!"

"Here they come!" called Hill from just above.

Yann followed the halfling's outstretched finger and spotted them, blurred and uncountable in the hot, shimmering air, but definitely there and definitely approaching.

He notched an arrow, aimed, and waited, knowing that above him Hill was doing the same.

The beasts came closer, and closer, and then split.

"Lord Warrior, you see the approaching column of flame-beasts divide into two columns, one of which is clearly slanting down towards you."

"This is not fair!"

"You think that they might have been alerted by the movement of your sword as you practice."

"It is still not fair. I am defenceless!"

"So is the monkey sentient, then?" asks the Jester.

"Damn the monkey! I am being attacked!"

"It might be. You don't know."

"Well I would have thought I would have bothered to find that out during the four hundred odd days I've had it?"

"Yes. I'd have thought that too."

"I demand that someone protect me!"

As it swooped down, it could sense that the cold one who healed was alone. It knew of being alone, for it had been alone once, when it had sickened, and drifted down towards the heavens below.

The cold ones that infested the cliff above it spat death from afar, but the lone cold one had never done this. It had healed once, from afar, long ago.

But the cold one healed no more. Comrade after comrade had fallen dying past it, hoping for the healing blast to jet out and wash across its body.

117

But no healing blast had come. There was only cold.

Much cold.

Cold that vigorously moved, and swirled, and pulsed.

It swooped down towards the cold one who'd healed, a string of pack mates following.

Closer, closer, closer.

Burning.

"The lead flame beast impales itself on your sword and explodes, throwing burning tar all over you, blinding you. Two more of the flame beasts slam into you in quick succession, showering you with more burning tar." The AllFather pauses for a moment. "You are now on fire."

"I'll lay down on the ledge and roll the fire out," the Warrior tells him.

"It is a bit narrow, I'm afraid. We'll have to consult the knuckle-bones to determine if you manage to remain on the ledge."

"There is a risk that in attempting to put out the fire I might roll off the edge of the ledge?"

"Yes."

"That is not fair!"

"I didn't say you can't do it. I just said that there is a risk that you might go over the edge."

"I cannot risk going over the edge. I will carefully lay down and then stay still."

"You do realise you're on fire?"

It was the most awesome thing Yann had ever seen, and the most terrible.

Three hundred feet below them, Draag lay on his back, motionless and engulfed in flame, but screaming defiance, his arms raised, as though daring the fire to do its worst.

Yann looked away. It was too terrible to watch.

Finally however, he sensed in the watching Hill's face that it was over. He looked back down and saw the dark paladin's body lying unmoving upon the ledge, scattered fires still burning upon its armoured surface.

The halfling shook his head. "He's gone."

Chapter Sixteen

It has already been established that the Universe has twelve and a half planes of existence.

This is not, strictly speaking, one of them.

The room is plain, with white walls, no windows and only two doors. A number of beige coloured sofas are randomly placed around the room, interspersed with several low, wooden, and equally randomly placed coffee tables, each of which is home to a selection of old and tattered magazines.

A figure crashes through the far door. He is dressed from head to foot in black, and blackened, armour.

He sits down on one of the sofas, picks up a magazine, flicks through it for a few moments, and then throws it down, sighing.

The door at the room's other end opens quietly, and a white clad figure walks through. The figure, who bears a welcoming smile and clutches a clipboard in his hand, glides serenely over to the armoured figure.

He is the Personnel Transit Manager, and his role in existence is, not surprisingly, to manage those personnel who are currently in transit from one plane of existence to another.

It's a job he has been carrying out since the start of eternity and he is, in his opinion, rather good at it.

He glides to a halt before the new arrival and draws himself up – but is then interrupted before he has a chance to speak.

"It's okay," says the newcomer, waving a hand but not bothering to look up. "I won't be staying."

"I know you won't be staying sir," says the Personnel Transit Manager through gritted teeth. "But we need to figure out where you are going to, don't we?"

He resists the temptation to fold his arms or frown and instead keeps the tight smile smiling. This is obviously going to be one of those difficult ones. That mortals can spend a lifetime believing in the afterlife and yet still get so upset at dying is a fact that has long amused him.

"Now I know this is all very traumatic for you, but denial helps no-one and the sooner you can accept what's happened to you the sooner we can get you sorted out."

He tries a warm smile. "We don't want to stay here for all eternity, do we love? So, let's look at what we've got for you and see if we can figure out where you're supposed to be going."

He scans through the first page of his clipboard, and flicks the page over. There is another page below that, and another below that, and another below that.

He flips through the pages, scanning through each one, tutting periodically.

"Oh dear. We have been a bad boy, haven't we?"

He gets no response. He tries the warm smile again. "Look, it's not so bad. If you're prepared to show a bit of repentance and a dash of remorse I might be able to get you into the tenth plane of existence, and if you do your time there, few slices of eternity and all that, you might be looking at a second chance in the mortal realm as..."

The armoured figure looks up at him, and stares a stare rendered blank by his metal faceplate.

"...as perhaps a hedgehog?"

The figure says nothing, but continues staring.

"Look, I know it's not much, but it's a start, and if we crunch the numbers we might be able to get you up as far as perhaps even a squirrel!"

Still the stare.

"Look, we can at least get something you can build on! And you do surely admit that you have been a very, very bad boy?"

The figure finally speaks. "You don't understand. I'm not staying. I'm going back."

"Going... back?"

"Look I've been here before and I know the routine. I won't be staying. So why don't you just get back to whatever it was you were doing and I'll just read some of your magazines."

The Personnel Transit Manager takes a fresh look at the newcomer, and realises that he does, in fact, look horribly, awfully, heart-sinkingly familiar.

"I'm afraid we've haven't got in any new magazines since you were last here," he snaps. "But I'm sure you can find something to occupy yourself with."

He glides away.

The OverRealm. The gods exchange stunned glances.

"So he's actually dead?" asks the Jester.

"That is not something your mortal knows," says the AllFather. "But he strongly suspects so."

"Oh well."

The AllFather looks across the table at the Warrior. "You appear to be taking this news with great equanimity, Lord Warrior?"

"It is but a temporary setback."

"I think you'll find it's a bit more permanent that that," says the Dealer.

"It is not. I have a potion of resurrection."

"Since when?" shout at least three of the figures around the table.

"Since the visit to the City. My mortal purchased the potion there in anticipation of the dangers that the journey might pose."

"You didn't mention it to me," protests the AllFather.

"No. Because you decided to skip through my mortal's visit to the City. Nonetheless, I updated the money and equipment sections of my mortal's life-slate accordingly."

He picks up the slate from in front of him and holds it up for the

AllFather to read (an action more symbolic than actual, given that the AllFather's eyesight is not what it once was). "See. It's written down!"

"Just because it's written down doesn't make it true," says the AllFather.

"And besides," says the Dealer. "I thought that after the last time we agreed on no more resurrections."

"We agreed on no such thing," says the Warrior. "It is you who had the problem with my last resurrection."

"Me who had a problem? You're the one who killed the priest thirty seconds after he bought you back.

"His price was unreasonable. That was my objection and in eliminating him I eliminated my objection. It is your problem that you are referring to, which is your distaste for the action I performed."

"Ripping out his heart and using it to smear blood across his altar?"

"Exactly."

The AllFather clears his throat. "Well even were I to accept that this potion has been bought..."

"You have to accept it! It is written on my mortal's life-slate!"

"All right. Fine. Your mortal has a potion of resurrection secreted away in a pocket somewhere!"

"Good. Thank you."

"But even allowing for the fact that your mortal does have a potion of resurrection, there is still the little problem of the fact that none of your late mortal's comrades have any knowledge of this."

The Jester laughs. "Yeah. We'll just tip your body off the ledge."

"And say a few words," adds the Dealer.

"You can say a few words if you want to. Me? I'm just tossing it into the void!"

The Warrior waits until the Jester has finished chuckling and then speaks. "This issue is one that the makers of the potion foresaw. It is all taken care of."

Hill slammed another magazine into the crossbow and immediately fired out a quick sequence of bursts.

Hit.

Hit.

Hit,

Miss.

Track, last burst.

Hit.

That last one had been bloody close, so close that its death explosion showered fragments of burning tar across them. Hill flicked a few burning embers off his leather armour and reached for a new magazine, already seeing a new attack force of flame-beasts arching in.

He was just raising the crossbow to his shoulder, his eye already focussing on the telescopic sight's cross-hairs, when something rising from below caught his eye.

It rose and swirled like smoke, but it glowed all the colours of the rainbow. It stopped, expanded, formed, the colours grouping and organising, until finally it formed into a solid and recognisable image.

Draag.

The image spoke, a voice that seemed to come from everywhere and nowhere, all at the same time.

"My dearest comrades."

"My dearest comrades?"
"It was a standard message. It would have cost extra to change it."

"If you are hearing this message, then it means that I have died. I know this will be something you'll find very distressing."

"You should have spent the extra."

"But fear not!"

"Who's fearing?"
"Oh do be quiet!" snaps the AllFather.

"For I am not gone, I am merely sleeping. In my pocket is a potion of resurrection. Simply pour that past my cold lips and life will return once more to my body. Somewhere my soul lies restless, for I purchased this potion knowing that I am not yet ready to begin the next cycle of life. Comrades, find my body, and give it the potion."

The voice stopped speaking.

Hill guessed the image had gone also, but he didn't actually know – he already had the crossbow to his shoulder and was firing out another sequence of bursts.

"What makes you think our mortals will want to bring you back?" asks the Jester.
"Great dangers await them and their quest could not have greater importance. As much as your mortals might not like mine, they will recognise their need for his sword-arm."
"Bugger. He's got us there."
"I'm still not happy about the whole concept of resurrection," says the Dealer. "It violates the entire cycle of existence, and devalues

the sanctity of mortal life! Bad enough to get a priest to do it, but to put it in a bottle and sell it..."

He looks around for support, but gets only awkward looks and embarrassed shrugs.

"I see I am alone in this," he mutters, bitter.

"We got more incoming!" Yann screamed. "Got a lot more incoming!"

Hill lifted his sighting eye from the telescopic sight, counted, and swore.

"You know, I'm starting to think they don't like us."

He thought for a moment, then reached down to click a switch on the side of the crossbow into its forward position, ignoring Yann's warning glance from below.

It was time to get serious.

He tracked the incoming column, waited, then squeezed the trigger–
–and held.

A long blaze of death spat out of the crossbow, a spread of fifteen bolts that tore into the flame-beasts and sent three - no four - of them spiralling down.

No time to think. Moving by instinct now, Hill ejected the spent magazine with one hand while reaching for a replacement with the other.

Aim, track, fire, hold.

He blazed through another full magazine, but still there were flame-beasts heading at him.

Eject.

Load.

Aim.

Fire.

Click.

The OverRealm.

The Jester stares in horror at the set of knuckle-bones that lay before him. There are many of them; but not one of them sits as he would like.

No successes.

"I warned you this might happen," says the Dealer.

The Jester waves protesting hands at the knuckle-bones. "Yeah, but how often would you expect something like that to happen!"

"About one out of every seven times."

The Jester shoots him a hard look, and then resumes his disbelieving staring.

The AllFather clears his throat. "What are you going to do?"

"Well there's not much I can do now, is there?"

"Well the flame-beasts are still heading in, and if you don't say something quickly I'm going to rule that your mortal is mentally paralysed by what's happened.

"Look I just think it's a bit mean—"

It all happened in slow motion, like one of those dreams where you're trying to run, but can't, and the more you struggle, the slower the world seems to go.

Hill remembered the click as the first bolt of the magazine jammed in the firing chamber. He remembered Yann's shouts from below, tinny and distorted as though shouted into the teeth of a hard winter's gale. And he remembered the flame beasts, approaching, slowly, growing larger, and larger, and larger.

Then there was only pain.

And blackness.

The AllFather consults first the knuckle-bones that lie before him, and then the notes scrawled upon his tablets.

The lead flame beast has impacted straight into your face, causing extensive burns and blinding you."

"Well that's just great! How long am I blinded for?"

The AllFather picks up his knuckle-bones, throws them again, peers at the result, consults his notes, peers at the knuckle-bones again, and emits a sound that sounds awfully like: "Ah."

"So how long then?"

"Well, for ever actually. You're blinded."

"I'm blind?"

"Yes."

"Can't see?"

"Yes."

"Well I'm going to make a pretty useless thief if I can't see, aren't I?"

"I thought you were a scout?" says the Lady.

"Whatever. Point is, I might as well be dead like him."

He points at the Warrior, and then thinks for a moment.

"If I died, and then took a resurrection potion, would I come back fully healed."

"No!" says the AllFather quickly, diving in before the Warrior can protest.

"Pity. So I'm totally blind then?"

"Yes."

"Nice."

The AllFather looks across at the Dealer. "You'll need to make a resolve test."

"Why?"

The Jester pastes on a fake smile. "Well I'm guessing it's something to do with the fact that I just tried to use a bucket's worth of molten tar as a facial treatment!"

The Dealer frowns, then sends his knuckle-bones across the table.

"But you could decide that resurrection is species specific?" says the Lady, pressing.

"Well, I suppose I could."

"And it would be awfully convenient in this case."

"Well yes."

The AllFather taps his fingers on the desk.

"Oh all right, fine. Resurrections are species specific."

The Jester holds his arms out in surrender. "Fine, right, okay. The dog's dead, gone, kaput. Departed to the doggy heaven from which there is no exit."

Tallenna looked down, at the ledge so far below, and felt a surge of sadness at what she saw: Hill and Shovel together, the dog's lifeless head resting one final time on his master's lap.

"It is for the best," the Warrior tells the Jester in a tone that attempts compassion but achieves only solemnity.

"Easy for you to say."

"Easy perhaps, but true also. The mission will have need of Draag's skills. That the potion has not now been wasted is a good thing."

The AllFather clears his throat. "That the potion has not now been wasted has not yet come to pass."

"I'm sorry?" says the Warrior, genuinely confused.

"Hill didn't know that the potion was human specific–"

"Human specific?" asks the Jester, interrupting. "I thought we'd just decided to discriminate against dogs. I didn't realise we'd decided to close off some of my options if ever I find myself biting the big one!"

"Do you have any potions of resurrection?"

"Well yes, perhaps. His one!"

"Well were you planning on dying any time soon?" snaps the AllFather.

"So help me, if this debate carries on much further I'll kill myself!" says the Lady.

"I'm just making the point!" says the Jester.

"Fine. We'll say the potion works on humanoids only. Happy?"

"Not really."

"Well tough!"

"No need to get snappy."

"I am not getting snappy."

It is because of times such as these that the AllFather long ago concluded that being a supreme being really isn't what it's cracked up to be. He takes a deep breath.

"The point is that Hill didn't know that the potion worked on humanoids only, and so would have given it to the dog, anyway."

The Warrior opens his mouth to speak, pauses, then closes it again, frowning.

Silence settles.

The Personnel Transit Manager has been doing this job since the start of eternity. Though his role might not be as glamorous as those of the Lords and Mistresses who inhabit what he jokingly refers to, in private, as "Upstairs", he knows that it is every bit as vital.

He has seen misery.

He has seen anger.

He has seen denial.

He has seen confusion.

But he has never seen anything like this. He stands beside the armoured newcomer, both of them staring at the dog which has, on several recent occasions, disappeared, and which they half expect to disappear once more.

The dog looks back at them.

"It was gone," the Personal Transit Manager says, vigorously pointing.

"It was," the newcomer agrees. "And then it was back."

"And then it was gone. Then back. And then... How many times did it happen? I just can't see how that sort of thing could happen?"

The newcomer sits down and stares hard at the wall, any thoughts he may have unspoken.

Or the gods or our ancestors talking to us. When we have such thoughts, we are sometimes wise to listen to them."

"Like when you somehow knew that we had to go to the Gate, and when we got there we found Draag waiting to be let in?"

"Exactly."

Tallenna shrugged. "Well I won't be able to enjoy my meal until then, so what the hell!" She lay down on the smooth rock, and edged forward to peer over the edge. "I'm not quite sure what I'm supposed to be looking for though!"

"Five successes," announces the Lady.

The AllFather nods. "At first you can see nothing save the endless expanse of the rock falling away below you. But then, far, far below, you pick out some small specks."

"How many?"

"Too many to count. Perhaps several score. It looks like they're spread out, some further away than others. The upper ones are falling straight away from you. But the lower ones are moving out away from the cliff-face."

"Moving out?"

"Yes."

The Jester clicks his fingers. "They're the flame beasts. Once they hit terminal velocity, it will take them about five hours before they reach the sea. And the combat was only about, what?"

"It started around about two hours ago," says the AllFather.

"How far down did you say the nostrils were?" asks the Lady.

"Yann believed that they were around four hundred miles down."

Yann said what Tallenna was thinking an instant before she had the chance to say it.

"It's the world-serpent. It's breathing out, and blowing them away from it. Which means..."

Tallenna looked at him. "Which means that if we time it right..."

"And jump..."

"We'll be sucked into the nostrils when it breathes in!"

The AllFather considers standing up and delivering a shouted "Hallelujah!" but decides upon reflection that this might be both undignified and insulting.

He instead allows himself a quiet smile and a small sigh of relief.

Yann peered at the tiny sparks of light below as the magical flares Tallenna had cast disappeared one by one into the void he knew to be the nostril. He continued looking for a further two minutes, then nodded, satisfied that his conclusions were valid.

"It is time" he announced. "The inhale is near peak flow and will be reaching its final stages in a little over two hours. We must jump now."

Tallenna nodded, her face the calm mask she wore at times of stress. Yann laid a hand on Hill's shoulder. "Are you ready brother?"

"No," the halfling replied. "But I might as well do it anyway. Least I won't have to worry about keeping my eyes shut."

Yann glanced down, at the body upon which Hill and Stone sat.

"You must give me the potion! You agreed!"

The Jester holds up a hand. "We agreed to give the potion at some point. We didn't discuss when."

"But if you leave Draag's body on the ledge then you will have no further chances. You must apply the potion now!"

The Jester smiles. "Relax. We're not going to leave Draag behind. Like you said, we'll most likely have need of him later on in the mission."

"Thank you."

Yann, spread his feet, taking the weight up his arms, through his shoulders, and down his back. He nodded at Stone. "Ready?"

Stone nodded.

"Okay," said Yann as they swung the weight back, and then forward. "One..."

High.

"Two..."

Higher.

"Three!"

Release.

The body sailed high into the air and then began its long fall. Yann wiped his hands and stepped back from the edge. "Okay, that's Draag sorted."

"I must protest! This is an undignified way to treat a warrior!"

The AllFather spreads his hands, a helpless expression on his face. "Perhaps, but it is what they have chosen to do. And they are correct in saying that the potion does not have to be applied immediately. As long as they keep the body with them, they can apply the potion whenever they choose."

The Warrior glares at his fellow gods. "And when will that be?"

The Jester shrugs. "I don't know. But whenever it is, we'll clearly be really, really desperate."

"Stone, you're next," said Yann.

"I'm sorry?" said Stone, confused.

"You're next to jump."

ice, as it were."

"Would Yann feel that way? I thought you placed being true to his inner spirit above all things? I would have thought that his sense of justice and honour would compel him to resurrect Draag straight away?"

"That is true," admits the Dealer. "But his sense of justice and honour would then compel him to challenge Draag to trial by combat, in order that the innocent lives he has shed be avenged. Yann would simply have to kill him."

"I'd help!" adds the Jester.

"But it's not very nice for Lord Warrior to have to sit and watch, is it?"

"That's Lord Warrior's reward for creating so objectionable a mortal," says the Lady. "I don't know why you invited him to join the game in the first place."

"Well I didn't quite invite him," says the AllFather. "He sort of invited himself, and I didn't feel able to say no. You know what he's like."

"Perhaps I can suggest a compromise," says the Dealer. "It might help if we advanced things forward a bit, to the point where our mortals might need to resurrect him."

"It would be good to just skip the nostrils and the sinuses and whatever the other stuff was, go straight to the brain, and do the thing with the healing whatnot," says the Jester.

"It's an elixir," says the AllFather.

The Jester thinks for a moment. "Hey! Would a bit of that cure my blindness?"

The AllFather gives him a whithering look. "It's designed for a near-immortal thirty-thousand mile long sea serpent. Your mortal is a three foot four long halfling. I suggest you consider those facts when pondering on that question. I further strongly suggest that you include the word 'no' on your short-list of possible answers."

"I was only asking. Anyway, I'm still with Lord Dealer. I could do without playing through six weeks trekking through tubes."

"I think you'll find that sinuses are much more than mere tubes!" says the AllFather pompously.

"In what way?" asks the Jester.

The AllFather realises that he may have driven himself into an embarrassing conversational cul-de-sac. He only put sinuses into his schema of creation because Mr Six Days had laughed at his original plans, saying that people's heads would explode if they ever went flying. Mr Six Days had then launched into an explanation, but it had been long and smug and complicated and had involved frequent use of the phrase "intelligent designer". When it had finally drawn to a close the AllFather had been too embarrassed to ask for a recap.

"They're just very special, okay?" he snaps.

"Okay. They're special. But can we still skip them?"

The AllFather looks down at the tablet before him, at the descriptions and encounters and conundrums that will now stay forever upon the scribed marble.

"Okay," he mutters sadly. "Perhaps someone can go and find Lord Warrior."

It had been a difficult journey, made more difficult by the load they'd had to drag, but now they were finally nearing their destination.

Yann nodded to Stone, and they dropped the Draag dragger. There had been frequent accidents in the early days, near-dislocated shoulders caused when one person dropped and the other did not, but now he, Stone and Hill were operating as a smooth well-oiled team.

The dragger dropped to the ground with a crash. The monkey, who'd been sleeping on the body's chest, bounced, slid down the side of the armour, and woke up in an angry chatter.

Yann ignored it and took out the map. Tallenna and Hill gathered round. "We're here," he said. "Past that bend is the beginnings of the brain, and the point where we can apply the elixir."

"Finally," breathed Tallenna.

Yann put the map away and then nodded to Stone. They picked up the Draag dragger and began moving forward. He could feel the excitement growing in all of them – Stone, perhaps, excepted – with every step they took. Around that corner was their destiny, a destiny that had been written nearly twenty thousand years before.

Around that corner was the immortality of legend.

Around that corner was the saving of an entire world.

Slowly, agonisingly, the corner was turned.

Around the corner was a door.

Chapter Twenty

"It's a door?" asks the Jester, interrupting.

"Yes. It's a door," says the AllFather. He begins to re-read his aborted description. "In front of you, the long cave-like sinus comes to a dead-end, the way forward blocked by a door. The door's surface is–"

"This is supposed to be a living creature!" says the Jester. "How in hell can there be a door?"

The AllFather considers making a third-attempt to read his description, but decides that the best way to treat the Jester's latest outburst is as a metaphorical question requiring no reply.

Silence thus resumes its reign as he waits for some kind of further response. Eventually, he gets one.

"It's a door?" asks the Dealer.

It's not much of a response, as responses go, but the AllFather feels it's something he can work with. "Yes," he says. "It's a door."

"A metal door?" asks the Lady.

"Yes. It's a metal door."

"As in refined metal, constructed metal, artificial metal?"

"Yes, yes and yes."

"And there's a small thick glass window in it?" asks the Dealer.

"Yes."

"And through the window we can see a long metal-lined corridor leading away from us?" asks the Lady.

"Yes."

"This is boring!" shouts the Warrior. "I would not have returned had I known it was for this."

"Well I happen to think this is an interesting challenge," says the AllFather.

"Draag was created for the challenge of combat, not the challenge of doors! We don't have to be here, you know!"

"True," says the Jester.

"There are other things we could be doing!"

"Well I do try to make this interesting for all of you!" protests the AllFather.

"Well you're not trying very hard!"

"I'm not particularly enjoying the whole blindness thing either, if anyone's keeping score," says the Jester.

The Lady gives him a scornful look. "Hard as it might be for you to comprehend, this universe was not created for the sole purpose of either your or our enjoyment."

"Well why was it created then? What purpose is there in creating a universe if it's not to play with the souls it contains?"

"That's sociopathic!"

"Better a sociopath than a psychopath!" says the Jester, nodding in the Warrior's direction.

"The door?" suggests the AllFather.

"I'm not sure what this all means," says the Dealer.

"I know what it means," says the Jester.

All heads turn quizzically towards him.

"It means the elves have completely screwed it up. They've spent twenty thousand years working towards the wrong sodding answer."

Hill knew from bitter past experience that picking a lock was a slow, painstaking task during which you had to allow your fingers to act as your eyes – which given that he was now a couple of eyeballs short of the expected total was currently rather convenient.

He just wished he was having more luck on the actual lock picking front. Quite frankly, after several weeks of clumsy sledge dragging and under-appreciated whining, his ego was in need of some gentle stroking and the last thing he'd wanted to encounter was the bastard lock from hell that he was currently failing to pick.

But eventually, he was forced to concede defeat, slumping back against the door and delivering his verdict.

"It's not a lock."

The next voice was Yann's. "What do you mean it's not a lock?"

"I mean it's not a lock as I understand the term. I'll concede the possibility that one day some geezer might walk up here with something he calls a key, shove that something into that there hole, and make the door open. But I can tell you this: that particular something wouldn't be something I'd recognise as a key."

"So you can't pick the lock." That was Tallenna.

"No."

Yann spoke. "We have to get through that door!"

"Why?"

"Because the world's going to end!"

"Maybe. Maybe not. Maybe we've got the wrong answer to the right question and maybe we've got the wrong answer to the wrong question but one thing I figure we haven't got is the right answer to the right question. If the door was open, I'd go through it. There ain't nothing that intrigues me more than a locked door, you know that."

"Because where there's locks there's loot?"

"Motto I've lived my life by, mate. But there's a big difference between a locked door you've unlocked and a locked door that's still locked, and that's that you can go through one and not the other."

Tallenna spoke. "So you would just go back then, would you?"

Hill shrugged. "It's a thought. Be a bloody long climb mind, followed by a bloody long walk."

The Warrior breaks the resulting silence with a strategic cough.

"I believe you had agreed to resurrect me when we reached our destination?"

"We did," says the Dealer.

"You have not yet resurrected me!"

"That's because we haven't got there yet," says the Jester, "on account of there being a damn great door in the way."

"Nonetheless. You have reached a destination, even if it was not the one you hoped for. I demand you keep your end of the bargain."

"He has got a point," says the AllFather.

"Look," says the Jester. "All he's going to do is punch the door, shoulder charge the door, and then flame the crap out of it."

"That is a grotesque over-simplification of the actions I intend to perform."

"Oh fine, whatever. I'll give him the sodding potion."

"You're blind."

The Lady sighs. "I'll give him the potion then."

For Draag, the change was both instantaneous and drawn out. One moment he was in the waiting room, reading the ingredients list on the side of a packet of headache tablets he'd found in a waste paper basket, the next he was no-where and yet somewhere.

A hard and roughened surface beneath him. A weight on his chest. A dark grey swirling in front of his eyes. Consciousness returned, slowly.

"Your vision is still very, very blurred," says the AllFather, "and you're completely unable to raise yourself into a sitting position. You can feel a huge pressure on your chest which is actually making breathing quite difficult."

The Warrior looks confused. "I will sweep my hands down and across my armour."

"They collide with something soft, something resting on top of your chest."

The Dealer waves a confused hand. "Sorry, is there something on top of him?"

"Well yes, of course. Stone is still using him as a sofa."

"Well you're just being stupid now!" shouts the Jester.

"I'm being stupid? You carry a body around for several weeks for no other purpose than to provide you with portable furniture and you say that I'm being stupid?"

An angry silence falls.

Finally, the Lady breaks the deadlock.

"Perhaps Stone should... stand up?"

The Sleeper looks up from his daze. "Oh! Okay. I'll stand up."

Ten minutes of furious activity had visibly changed the door. Where before it had been smooth and shiny it was now blackened and covered in soot.

Other than that, it looked to Tallenna like pretty much the same door it had always been.

Draag stepped back snarling, and returned DeathSinger to its scabbard.

"It appears to be impenetrable," he said.

"Could have told you that," muttered Hill.

"All options should be examined! You are upset because you were unable to pick the lock."

"It's not a lock!"

"It's got a hole."

Tallenna would have been happy to just let them get on with it, but Yann stepped in between them. "Arguing isn't going to help."

"It's something to do," said Hill, shrugging.

"I achieved as much as you achieved and in a third of the time!"

"I really wish we could put him back in his box," muttered Hill to no-one in particular.

"So," said Yann, "what was heaven like? My people have many theories."

"Boring."

"Boring?"

"Yes. The magazine selection was poor and there were not enough of them. And they hadn't got any new ones in since last time."

It was at times like this that Tallenna was glad to be an agnostic, that is one who accepted the existence of the gods but did not particularly feel that any of them were worthy of her worship. Yann though looked more troubled at this revelation.

"Magazines?"

It occurs to the AllFather that silence is the natural state of the table, and that it is the brief moments of play that are the intruders.

He is still thinking on this point when the Dealer finally manages to deliver the question his mouth has been attempting to deliver for some considerable time now.

"So, there's just a door?"

Sometimes a question long prepared ends up being not the one you were preparing, but something, anything, that comes to mind when you realise you can't think of a question. The AllFather suspects this to be the case with the question the Dealer has just delivered.

However, in this case, the question might have blindly stumbled onto the start of the correct track. It occurs to the AllFather that he has perhaps fallen into a petty approach to this encounter, but he quickly quashes this thought. After all, he can only guide his players to the extent they are prepared to be guided.

"Define just?" he says.

The Dealer looks at him suspiciously. "Is the door simply a door and nothing more?"

"It is."

The Dealer looks confused. Then the Jester breaks in. "Hang on, he's playing word games. You didn't ask if it, the door, was just a door. You asked if there was just a door." He fixes his attention on the AllFather. "Is there anything here, other than us, the monkey, our equipment, the door, and rock."

"Well there is a small button beside the door."

"What?" shout the Dealer, the Jester and the Warrior simultaneously.

"Do you not think that perhaps you should have mentioned that?" says the Lady.

"You didn't ask," says the AllFather, who is actually thinking that perhaps he should have mentioned it.

"We didn't think we had to!" says the Jester. "You gave a description."

"Which you interrupted!"

"Yeah, but still, you should have mentioned it as something we could see!"

"It's a small button."

"Clearly!"

It was now five minutes since Hill had pointed out the small button sitting on the rock beside the door and in that time it had been the focus of much conversation, the principle theme of which was, of course, whether or not to push it.

"I say we press it!" said Draag.

"But we don't know what it will do," said Yann.

"That is irrelevant. We can talk all we like, but in the end the button is the only option available to us save humiliating retreat."

"Hate to admit it, but I'm with psycho here," said Hill.

"If it opens the door then we pass through. If it summons an occupant, we can kill the occupant and pass through. Either way, we pass through."

"Can I rescind my previous vote of support?"

"How about we just press the button and see what happens?" said Tallenna.

"Works for me," said Hill.

Draag nodded as, eventually, did Yann.

Tallenna pressed the button.

Nothing happened.

"So absolutely nothing happened when I pressed the button?" says the Lady.

"Well the button went in when you pressed it, and then popped back out when you released it," says the AllFather. "Other than that, nothing."

   "No clicks?" asks the Jester.

   "No sound at all."

   "I push the button again."

   "Okay. You've pushed the button."

   "Anything happen?"

   "No."

   "I shall push at the door," says the Warrior. "Does it open?"

   "No."

   "I shall charge it. It might be open but stiff!"

The doorbell had not been rung in more than forty thousand years, and it was therefore an extreme application of sod's law that whoever had just now rung it chose to do so not only during Guevarra's shift, but right in the middle of a quick, and technically rules-breaking, toilet break.

   "Alright, alright!" he shouted when the chime rang a second time. He pulled up his tunic and headed off down the corridor to the door, fabric flapping as he did up his buttons one by one.

   "Look! Nothing's happening!" shouts the AllFather, frustration evident in both his voice and his manner.

   "Then I'll try again! The door will yield!"

   "How many times have you tried so far?" asks the Jester.

   The AllFather looks down at the tallymarks on the tablet before him. "Twelve times."

   "Then I shall try a thirteenth!"

   The AllFather picks up his knuckle-bones and casts them across the table.

   "Finally!" says the Warrior. "It is about time that you test the door's strength."

   "What makes you think the knuckle-bones are for the door?" says the AllFather. "It's a luck test, actually."

   The Jester peers at the result and shakes his head. "Looks like someone's about to get very, very unlucky."

Guevarra had often looked through the thick narrow window that lay at the door's centre, snout pressed hard against the glass to get the best possible view. All those previous times there'd been nothing to see save a rock lined passageway unchanged for forty thousand years.

But not now.

Because someone, something, had rung the doorbell.

His hearts bursting with the possibilities of what he might see, he pressed his snout hard against the glass, just in time to see a large black mass thud into the door from the other side.

Pain.

Blackness.

A sound arrived from the other side of the door. It was muffled, and indistinct, but it sounded to Hill's sensitive ears like a cry.

"Did you guys hear something?" he asked.

"Yes," said Yann. "Draag charging the door."

Draag crashed into the door, again. It vibrated and emitted a dull clang, but again it held.

"No, something else. A cry."

"Well I didn't hear anything," said Yann, shrugging.

Draag draw himself back to make another charge, but Hill dived in front of him and lined himself up with the narrow window slot.

"What can I see?"
"Nothing. You're blind."
"I'll take a look then," says the Dealer.

"What can you see?" asked Hill, jogging up against Yann.

"I can see something, someone lying there, on the floor."

"Something? Well what does it look like?"

"What does the figure look like?" asks the Dealer.

"It's some kind of lizard."

"Well what's it doing?"

"What's it doing?" asks the Dealer.

The AllFather passes a small tablet across the table, to join the collection already sitting in front of the Dealer.

The Dealer picks it up and reads it. "It appears to be unconscious."

The Jester sighs theatrically. "Look can we stop with the notes and just take it as read that Yann's telling me what he's seeing?"

"Can we trust you to not conveniently forget that you're blind?"

"Just because I've forgotten once or twice!"

The AllFather says nothing but merely raises an eyebrow.

"Okay, okay! You can trust me!"

"Thank you. Now as I was saying, there is a figure lying apparently unconscious on the other side of the door. It's humanoid, but looks lizard-like."

"Lizard-like?" asks the Lady.

"Its skin is green, with scales, its eyes are yellow with slitted pupils, and it has a forked tongue."

"What? Is it flicking the tongue at us or something?" asks the Jester.

155

"No. It's unconscious. Its tongue's hanging out of its mouth."

"Does it look intelligent?"

"Well it's wearing clothes and it has some kind of thin metal rod in its hand that looks awfully like a manufactured artefact."

"That will be the key!" says the Warrior.

"It's not a lock, okay?"

"If you insist."

"I don't have to insist, it's a fact."

"If you say so."

"The lizard?" says the AllFather.

"Perhaps we should wait for it to wake up," says the Lady.

"That's assuming it's not dead," says the Dealer.

The Warrior leans forward. "Perhaps we should try pushing the button again?"

Guevarra regained consciousness to the sound of the doorbell ringing. He could sense wetness on his snout; he wiped with a claw and it came away green. Blood.

The doorbell rang again. Twice.

He pushed himself upright, his head swirling, and again approached the door, warily this time. He considered looking through the window again, but this time did not.

His job was not to look at the arrivals.

His job was simply to open the door.

And besides, his snout was still hurting like hell.

He inserted the key into the lock, and the door slowly opened towards him, forty-thousand years of inactivity breaking in one long echoing grind.

The two figures standing just the other side of the door greeted him with smiles, waves, and melodic but incomprehensible speech.

"Drzzzzit qkxxxrt!"

The tales of the Makers were old now, and perhaps confused through more than a thousand and a half generations of retelling, but in those tales the Makers had spoken, and his people had understood. Perhaps these were not the Makers? But if that were so, why had they come to the Makers' door?

There were others standing beside the first two, and Guevarra examined them carefully. Two of them were like the nearer two who'd greeted him; pale, pink-coloured, scale-less skin with no shine, and a mess of flexible protrusions on the head.

The fifth figure had skin which had the smooth sheen of Guevarra's, but was a single shade of black and made of huge scales a foot or more across.

The final figure was the smallest: a tiny figure entirely covered with the protrusions that sat on its haunches at the back of the group.

The smaller of the two foremost visitors spoke again.

"Rftyyyyew jiqqqqsssd? Llfeeeesa iyvvvvvvs?"

"I'm very sorry," said Guevarra. "But I don't understand you. My duty now is to take you to the Chief Controller. Do you understand what I am saying?"

The smaller figure spoke again, louder this time. "Rftyyyyew jiqqqqsssd! Llfeeeesa iyvvvvvvs!"

In days gone by, those who manned the door and greeted the Makers were envied and admired and were drawn from the cream of society. But as millennia passed without visitations from the Makers, the job had become less prestigious, and the training more by rote and routine. Guevarra would not claim, if forced, to be drawn from the cream of his society, nor would he claim that his concentration during his training programmes had been all that it might have been.

And the fact that his head was still thumping wasn't helping things.

All of these were factors he now strongly regretted. He desperately wracked his misfiring brain for some relevant details – and then it hit him!

The signs the Makers had taught his people that they might communicate when background noise prevented speech!

He formed his hands into a half-remembered sign.

HELLO.

At first he saw only the same blank incomprehension that his attempts at verbal communication had produced. But no! One of those visitors behind the foremost two had the light of recognition in its eyes.

It signed; sign after sign that came far too fast for Guevarra's rusty memory.

He tried another sign.

SLOW.

The reply came again, slower this time, some signs incomprehensible, some barely recognisable.

THANK [SOMETHING]. GET ME AWAY FROM THESE [SOMETHING]. I WILL GIVE YOU [SOMETHING] THINGS.

Guevarra gulped. This was definitely one to dump in the Chief Controller's lap.

I WILL TAKE YOU TO MY LEADER.

The smaller one who previously greeted him stepped forward smiling.

"Rftyyyyew jiqqqqsssd? Llfeeeesa iyvvvvvvs?"

157

Chapter Twenty One

"So at what point," asks the Jester, "was someone going to bother to mention to me that he was talking to my monkey?"

"They were using sign language and you're blind," says the AllFather. "So the only way you were going to know was if one of them told you, and they didn't. So blame them!"

The Jester turns his head, and looks pointedly at the Dealer.

The Dealer points at the tablet sitting in front of the Jester. "Hey, he gave each one of us a tablet, including you. You didn't tell us what your one said."

The Jester grits his teeth. "That's because mine said, and I quote: everyone's stopped talking."

"You should have said something."

"I did!"

The Dealer pulls a helpless expression.

"Anyway," says the AllFather. "The lizard is beckoning you all to follow him down the hallway."

"I guess we should go," says the Jester.

"Is there anything any of you wants to do first, before you follow the lizard wherever it is he wants to take you?" asks the AllFather. He quickly scans through the notes on the tablet that sits on his lap, familiarising himself with what Takes has learned and is capable of telling the mortals.

"I still say we should kill the lizard and explore the complex ourselves!" says the Warrior.

"You know, next time you die I'm stuffing you in a lead lined coffin and nailing the lid shut with six inch spikes," says the Jester.

The AllFather tries one final hint. "The monkey is already heading through the door."

"Bloody traitor!" says the Jester. "That thing just doesn't understand the concept of loyalty.

"So where does he take us?" asks the Dealer.

"I'm spending the journey looking for any threats!" says the Warrior.

"And I'm looking out for any valuable looking stuff," adds the Jester.

The AllFather sighs, and gently places the tablet on the floor where it sits atop of stack of similarly discarded tablets.

He looks at the heading at the top of the tablet that sat underneath it and which he has now bought to the fore. The words are plain and unadorned, but they are words which the AllFather has been guiding events towards for more than twenty thousand of the mortals' years.

The Control Room.

The lizard paused in front of a set of doors, turned, spread his arms wide, and spoke, awe and pride clear in every syllable.

"Kjjjeewds heuuuuss gwqqqqd lllkrty!"

Tallenna smiled politely, a politeness that was genuine, and not a false mask. Whatever it was that they were about to see, she believed it would be wondrous, for had they not already seen wonders?

Their journey from the door had taken them into rooms which moved upwards and rooms which moved sideways. She suspected that they might have travelled hundreds, perhaps thousands, of miles. Corridor after corridor, cavern after cavern, void after void, all lined with the same unmarked metal.

Machines the size of cities, maintained by an ant-like army of lizards more numerous than even the City's teaming masses. Millions might dwell in these underground realms inside the head of the world serpent.

What were they doing?

What was their purpose?

And then the doors opened and in an instant Tallenna knew.

All his life Draag had craved not the power that people believed was his life's desire, but control, for was not control the most important thing in the universe? Control over oneself; control over one's environment; control over one's companions; control over one's enemies.

Draag was not stupid. People, lesser people, mistook his iron focus for dull stupidity; they usually lived only long enough to appreciate their mistake. Draag knew what he wanted, and knew it when he saw it.

He wanted control.

And then the doors opened, and control was what he saw. A greater possibility of control than he had ever dreamed existed. Control almost beyond comprehension.

Control that he aimed to make his.

All his life Yann had studied the night sky, watching the eternal dance of the stars overhead and seeking to understand what it might mean.

And then the doors opened.

Now, perhaps, he understood. Somewhere within his being he knew that he would never again be able to find solace in the night sky.

For he had seen the dance.

And the dancers.

Hill couldn't see a sodding thing.

All his ears had thus far managed to convey to him was more cheerful incomprehensibility from the lizard followed by a round of awed sighs from his companions.

"Bit of explanation be appreciated over here," he said quietly out of the side of his mouth.

"It's incredible," he heard Tallenna say in reply.

"It is... incredible," he heard Draag say.

"It is beyond anything I could have ever imagined or feared," he heard Yann say.

Hill considered this for a moment.

"Could you be just a little more specific?"

The AllFather gives the Jester a warning glance and then begins to read from the tablet in front of him.

"The door opens to reveal a large round room, most of whose circumference is lined with chairs in front of which sit panels speckled with jewelled flashing lights. Humanoid lizards much like the one who bought you here sit at each chair, wearing clothing that is similar save for the red flashes on each shoulder."

He takes a breath, and then continues reading. "At the centre of the room is a large chair, which appears to swivel, for at the moment it and its occupant are facing you. At the far end of the room..."

He pauses.

"What?" asks the Jester.

"Now remember. You're not actually seeing this, and this description represents what Yann and Tallenna are telling you. I'm just reading it out now to give the others a recap also."

The Jester waves a hand. "Yeah, yeah, whatever."

"At the far end of the room is a large window, beyond which is something that looks remarkably like the inside of an eye, a pupil surrounded by an iris. And beyond that... beyond that you can see the sky with the sun hanging low it in, and the rest of the universe beyond that."

The AllFather pauses once more. "In front of the screen is a long desk, covered in writing and lights. Two chairs sit behind it, facing the screen. A stick extends from the desk in front of the right-hand chair. The lizard sitting at that chair has his hand upon the stick and is watching the sun. The lizard in the central chair waves a hand. He seems to be motioning you to enter."

The lizard who'd sat in the central chair - a leader of some kind, Yann guessed - showed justifiable pride as he showed them round his realm.

He stopped beside the pair of lizards who sat before the main viewing window, and pointed first at the sun, and then at the stick. The lizard who gripped the stick nudged it a near imperceptible amount to the left, the third such movement Yann had noticed him make.

The leader spoke some more incomprehensibility, then made some signs at the monkey, which then looked at Yann and shrugged.

It didn't matter. The truth of the world was plain.

"This is some kind of control room," he said to Tallenna.

She nodded. "This is their purpose: to drive the world serpent as though it were a cart, eternally chasing the sun."

"The world is not what I thought it was," said Yann sadly.

"The world is what it always was," said the listening Draag, ever the pragmatist. "But now we know the truth. And we understand the power." He pointed at the controlling stick. "That stick controls the sun."

"You speak like you want to control that stick."

"I do. Who would not?"

Julen had been a fisherman all his life, as had his father before him, and his father before that.

The day's take had been good; his boat, the Alia Rayne, sat low in the water such was the weight of his catch. Tonight his wife and children would sleep with full bellies and the contentment of money in the cash-pot.

Julen pulled on the oars, letting the boat surf ahead of the incoming tide, riding the swell towards home, towards the village that nestled between the beach and the cliff.

A roaring roused him from his thoughts. He looked up, and saw a line of white on the horizon. A wave, impossibly high. Within seconds it was upon him, lifting his boat higher than it had ever been before. For a moment he saw all creation laid out before him, the village somehow below him, tiny and perfect - and then he was sliding down the wave's far face.

The wave crashed upon the shore, splashing up the face of the cliff and even onto the grassy tops beyond. For minutes the water gurgled and swirled until finally it retreated, leaving nothing behind.

The village was gone. The wave had taken it. Every single brick and every single soul.

The control room leader reached across, slapped Draag sharply across the knuckles, and shouted angrily.

Draag let go of the stick and withdrew his hand, the tilt of his armoured head suggesting a hurt glare. The lizard pilot gingerly eased the stick back from the hard-right angle to which Draag had rammed it. On the giant screen, the sun moved back to its central position.

"I was just having a go," said Draag.

The leader spat a further set of angry syllables. Yann didn't understand the precise meaning, but the guy was clearly incredibly pissed off. It was imperative that they establish communications. The success of their mission, and the fate of the world depended upon it.

Yann gave the monkey a suggestive prod.

It prodded him back.

"Can I make a suggestion?" said Hill.

"What?" says the AllFather, wearily.

"You haven't even heard what I'm going to say yet?" says the Jester.

"I apologise. What's your suggestion?"

"I don't know. I've forgotten it now."

"Perhaps we should just let the head lizard finish his tour?" suggests the Lady.

"Well you do notice that he seems rather keen to get you away from the controls," says the AllFather, sending a quick glare in the Warrior's direction.

"Can I see anything valuable?" asks the Jester.

"Was that your suggestion?"

"No. This just came to me."

"Right."

"So can I?"

"Can you what?"

"Can I see anything valuable?"

"No. You can't see anything. At all."

The Jester sighs. "Well can I feel anything valuable?"

"Are you feeling around?" asks the AllFather sarcastically.

"Yes."

"Well feeling around, the material that the desk is made out of feels smooth, almost like marble." He consults his notes for a moment, then looks back up. "Could you do an observation test please."

The Jester picks up his knuckle-bones. "How many successes do I need?"

"Twenty. Observation isn't a strong point of yours right now."

The control room leader had already been pretty angry, but Hill's blind fumbling around the control desk seemed to push him over the edge into an apocalyptic rage that started with a forearm chop to Hill's searching hand that Hill literally never saw coming and then segued into a neat backhand smash to the face that sent him tumbling back across the room.

Several sets of knuckle-bones bounce every which way across the table as four gods make initiative tests on behalf of their mortals.

"What are you doing?" asks the AllFather, genuinely confused.

"Casting for initiative!" says the Warrior. "Combat has started! We must determine who shall have the next action. We, or they!"

"Nothing's started!" protests the AllFather. "The head controller hit Hill because Hill was feeling around the control panel. This isn't a battle! You know, you could actually try talking to him?"

The gods trade glances, pondering this new possibility.

The Warrior points at his knuckle-bones. "The lizard can say what he wishes, but he needs to get more than seven successes if he wishes to say it before I react to his attack on Hill!"

The AllFather sighs. "You have the initiative. What do you wish to do?"

"I am pulling DeathSinger from its sheath and swinging it at him in one fluid movement, using all of Draag's inner resources of courage and resolve."

He scoops up the knuckle-bones and sends them bouncing across the table. "Nine successes!"

"Your sword cleaves through the head controller's neck," says the AllFather in a flat voice, "sending his now-lifeless head tumbling across the room. His body staggers once, twice, a fountain of blood jetting out of its severed neck, and then crashes to the ground." He pauses for a moment, and then looks at the Jester. "What are you doing?"

"Running!"

"In which direction?"

"Towards the door!"

"Which way's that?"

"Ah."

Chapter Twenty Two

On a spring day some thirty-seven years ago, Hill had participated in an interesting game that involved a blindfold, some leather, a pot of whipped cream, and a pixie girl who turned out to be a complete psycho.

All his memories of that "interesting" day of years ago were still fresh and immediate; but the memory that surfaced now was crystal clear in its clarity and intensity, painfully so in fact.

It was the memory of that precise moment when he'd not only realised that she intended to play a very different game than the one he'd been envisaging, but had further realised that given that he was the one who was blindfolded and tied to the bed, it was her wishes that the universe was likely to favour.

Terror is a much maligned and often underrated emotion. Terror of death is what drives men to survive hurricanes. Terror of financial ruin is what drives men to work impossible hours. Terror was what got a bound and blindfolded Hill out of the psycho pixie's bed.

And raw, screaming, absolute terror was what got Hill out of the control room.

"You've managed to unscrew the grate cover from the wall and have crawled inside the ventilation duct. It's only about eighteen inches square but that's plenty enough for you. There's an awful lot of noise and screaming behind you. What do you want to do?"
"I'll carry on crawling," says the Jester.
"But you don't know where it goes," says the Lady.
"Wherever it is, it's got to be better than here."

The interior of the control room looked like a slaughter house. Of the fifteen unarmed personnel who Yann estimated had been present when the battle began, seven were now killed and a further four wounded, two gravely. Three lizards were trapped in one corner; one had apparently escaped.

"Surrender or die!" screamed Draag at the three cowering lizards, before charging in and cutting them to pieces. He wiped DeathSinger on one of the bodies and returned it to its sheath. "Well that showed them," he announced.

Yann pointed at the control stick, now unmanned. "Who will drive the world serpent now that you have killed its controllers?"

Draag shrugged. "Worry not. They will be operating on a rotating shift system with five sets of controllers performing three eight-hour shifts. They'll just have to adjust the shift pattern temporarily while they train new workers."

Tallenna walked over to them, hazy beneath her shimmering force shield.

"Perhaps we ought to leave. Now. Before reinforcements arrive."

Yann nodded. He looked around. Someone was missing.

"Where's Hill?"

Tallenna looked around. "Not here. And the monkey's gone as well."

"We cannot go without him."

Draag slapped him on the back. "The halfling can look after himself, as can the monkey. We must march!"

Tallenna rested a hand on his shoulder. "Hill's obviously made his own escape. We'll search for him. But we have to leave. Now!"

It seemed to Hill like he'd been crawling for hours. His knees burned and his back ached and still the shaft continued its relentless forward course.

He stopped for a moment to catch his breath, the first stop he'd dared make since escaping the carnage of the control room. Something small and furry cannoned into his backside.

Hill had once heard a human use the expression "like a knife fight in a privy". He'd never felt much need for such wordage; his visits to a human privy generally involved a climb onto the pot after all. But the expression seemed apt now.

After a fair bit of scratching and biting, a good deal of which came from Hill's side of the conflict, he managed to get his miniature opponent into an improvised but emphatic underarm lock.

"Stop. Bloody. Wriggling," he told it.

It stopped, but only long enough to jab a tiny finger into one of Hill's ruined eyes.

"You sod!" Hill screamed. He twisted round to get a better grip on it, in the process pushing himself a further six inches along the shaft and across some kind of edge. He felt himself sliding, let go of his attacker, grabbed at something, anything, missed whatever it was that he might have been grabbing for, and fell into the void.

One hurried exit, two arguments, and one flight of stairs later, Tallenna and her three companions found themselves running along yet another long unmarked metallic corridor lined at intervals with grill-covered vents.

One screamed as they passed it, a long echoing cry that began with "iiiiii" and ended with "tttttttt", fading to silence as though falling away.

The corridor led them to a junction, three impossibly long tunnels stretching away to infinity, and in each of those tunnels was an army of angry lizards advancing upon them with metal blades in their hands.

Tallenna turned, ready to retrace her steps, but found a similar army advancing down the corridor along which they'd just run. She raised her arms and called upon the magic.

Forces of the universe, protect me from danger, shield me from harm.

The magic flowed.

Some time later, Hill crashed down into something that was soft and wet and which exploded from the force of his impact. He ripped straight through it into something squidgy that smelt like the devil's armpits, and there, choking and unable to breathe, his fall ended.

His hands clawed at the soggy, clammy debris that covered him, with only one purpose, one desire: air. After several desperate seconds of struggle his face pushed free and he breathed deeply. The air wasn't freshly smelling by even the most liberal standards, but it was air, and right then that was enough to make it feel very, very good.

For the first time since escaping the control room, Hill let himself relax for a moment.

"You can sense the mass of material around you moving," says the AllFather.

"Moving? You saying there's something alive in here?"

Yann looked down each corridor in turn and saw only thick wall-to-wall masses of figures.

"We're trapped," he said.

Tallenna, standing beside him, sheathed in crimson energy, nodded, whilst Draag merely snarled and tightened his grip on DeathSinger.

"I shall burn a way through," he growled.

Yann placed a hand on his arm, gently pushing his aim downward. "There has been enough killing."

"Do you expect me to surrender?" asks the Warrior.

"I don't expect you to do anything," says the Dealer. "But if you fight, I shall not be alongside you, even though your action will most likely doom us all."

The Lady nods in agreement.

The Warrior gesticulates angrily, hands flailing in the direction of the AllFather. "You are allowing him to railroad us! He has deliberately created a situation in which submission is our only course of action!"

"How is it I who created the situation?" asks the AllFather. "I was not the one who slaughtered the occupants of the control room."

"That battle was initiated by the head of the lizards!"

"That's true!" says the Jester. "He swiped me one!"

"Because you were feeling around the controls."

"Oh yeah, fair point."

"If we surrender they may kill us."

"If we don't they'll definitely kill us."

The Warrior pushes his chair back in frustration and folds his arms. "Fine. Do it your way then!"

Very slowly, Hill half crawled and half swam across the top of the sodden debris searching for an exit, or failing that, a wall.

He eased cautiously forward, and felt a shifting. Movement? Or just the surface giving under his weight? He paused, and felt another shifting. It was movement, he realised, fighting the panic rising within him. He crawled, reckless now, just wanting to be somewhere, anywhere, other than this.

His hand slipped, crashed down through a void, and pushed hard into something wet and warm and horrible. He kicked hard and it came free, and then something was upon him, pulling at his feet, and then flipping him onto his back.

He struck wildly, feeling his fists connect with cold solid flesh, but it had him, one limb held across his neck while the other probed his face. Claws brushed his skin, found an eye, and then it was digging, clawing into the socket, pushing, pulling.

Hill screamed.

And could see.

A lizard's face hovered inches above Hill's. "Are you okay?" it asked.

Hill pulled himself onto a dry looking ledge, and then extended a hand down to the lizard to help pull him clear of the evil-smelling gloop.

The lizard pulled a tooth-filled expression that Hill suspected, and certainly hoped, was a smile. "My name is Yrttttt."

Hill waved a weak hand. "Hillby Bigfella." He looked around. They appeared to be in a windowless metal room that measured around five yards by three and that save for the ledge was entirely filled by a semi-liquid swamp of... stuff.

"What is this place?" he asked.

"It is a garbage dump, Hillbybigfella," the lizard replied. His voice was somehow metallic, but still clear and understandable.

"Nice," said Hill, absently, as a thought occurred to him. "How come I can understand you?"

The lizard lifted up the metal hoop it wore around its neck. "This device translates your speech into mine and mine into yours."

Hill did a quick mental calculation and came up with a figure in excess of one hundred thousand gold crowns.

"Neat," he said, making a mental note.

"And how come I can see now? Are you a wizard?"

"He'll have used some kind of healing device," says the Lady.

The Warrior nods. "This entire civilisation is based on machines and technology in a way that exactly opposites the magical realm our mortals come from. For creatures such as these, the technology to restore sight would be trivial."

"You had something in your eye," said the lizard. "Look there's still something in the other eye." He pinned Hill to the ledge and forced a claw into his other eye socket.

Hill screamed, but stopped, embarrassed, when his field of vision widened and he saw the finger retreating, something small balanced on a claw.

"See?" said the lizard, showing the object to Hill. "You had one of these in each of your eyes."

It was a small round blackened disk.

"What?" shouts the Jester. "You're telling me that my eyes have been fine all along but my contacts had gone black?"

"Yes," says the AllFather. "Your contact lenses of eagle's sight took the full force of the flame-beast's assault, saving your eyes, but were themselves destroyed."

The Jester leans slowly, deliberately, forward, and speaks in a low, controlled voice. "Is that not something I might have noticed when I took the contacts off?"

"When would you have taken them off? Your mortal has had them for four years now and has worn them continuously for that entire period."

"No he hasn't. He takes them out every night."

"You have never told me that you were having him do that, not even once."

"I've never told you he was taking a piss but he isn't standing around with his legs crossed!"

"Well you never actually said it!" snaps the AllFather, who had, frankly, thought that the restoration of Hill's sight might actually be something the Jester would appreciate.

"Well I'm saying it now!"

"Fine!"

Hill breathed a sigh of relief as his bladder emptied in a long stream of urine that splashed onto the steaming garbage below. The jet was still flowing when he suddenly realised two things.

He had no idea what urge had possessed him to simply stand up and urinate.

The lizard was watching with some curiosity.

Hill quickly forced the last of the jet out, shook quickly, and tucked himself back into his breeches.

"Sorry about that!"

"Do you not think that was a little bit childish?" asks the Jester.

The AllFather is not quite sure how to answer this. He vacillates between the two possible answers of yes and no and eventually settles on the poor compromise of an unconvincing no, followed by: "Anyway, you're still standing on a ledge in a rubbish filled room with the lizard who's just rescued you."

"They could still use technology," says the Warrior, a little sadly.

The AllFather had been rather pleased with his idea of using the contacts to dig his game out of the hole his players had driven it into, a hole in which only one mortal was still at liberty and he was the one who was blind. He'd thought it a clever and original improvisation. He's not so sure now.

The Jester sighs. "Fine. Whatever. I guess we'd better get this train back on track." He puts on a exaggerated face and then speaks in a voice exaggerated to match.

"Take me to your leader!"

The lizard looked at Hill, confused. "I'm sorry, but I don't understand you."

"So much for the talk-talk machine!" The Jester looks at the AllFather. "I'll say it again, but more slowly."

"No. I understand the meaning of your words, but not the meaning of what you say. I cannot take you anywhere. If I knew how to leave this place then I would not have been here when you fell down the shaft to join me."

"You didn't come here to rescue me?"

"I did not know of your existence."

"So why were you here?"

"Like you, I was expelled from the above world and sent down the shaft to this place."

"Are you saying someone threw you down the shaft?"

The lizard looked at Hill, surprised. "Yes. Why else would one fall down the shaft?"

Hill shrugged, embarrassed. "Well you know, accidents happen. So why did they throw you down the shaft?"

"It is complicated. I still do not fully understand, even though I have had plenty of time in this place to try and complete my understanding."

"Well how long have you been down here?"

"More than one hundred shift cycles. It has been very hard."

Hill rested a friendly hand on his shoulder. "Well look around and tell this dump goodbye Yrttttt my old mate, because this is the last shift cycle you're spending here. The room ain't been built that can keep me in it!"

169

Chapter Twenty Three

During Hill's seven and a half minute fall down the shaft to the garbage dump he'd descended more than 120,000 feet, or to put it in more descriptive terms, around 10,000 storeys. He hadn't realised this at the time of course; quite frankly he'd most likely have lost count within the first few storeys even if he hadn't have been blind at the time.

No, the reason Hill knew just how many storeys he'd descended was because having made the outward journey at a speed of around one hundred and eighty miles per hour, he had to make the return climb at a somewhat more conservative rate of a thousand storeys a day, and this time round he was counting.

You learn a lot when you spend ten days alone with another person, be that person man, halfling, or lizard. It's not always useful and it's often not even interesting, but when the alternative is "I spy with my little eye, something beginning with m," learning anything is better than nothing.

"So let me get this straight," says the Jester. "The lizards have a religion that involves worshipping some beings they call the Makers."

"Yes."

"And Yrttttt is a follower of a minority sect of that religion, a sect whose followers are persecuted by the majority."

"Yes."

"And when he was discovered to be a member of that sect, he was thrown down the shaft as a sort of execution stroke exile."

"Yes."

"This is not fair!" says the Warrior. "He is monopolising table time. You should return the action to us!"

"Okay," says the AllFather. "You are still in the prison cell that the lizards took you to when they captured you three days ago. It is still a small, metal, windowless room with a metal floor, a metal ceiling, and a solid metal door. What do you want to do?"

"I will try the door again."

"It's still locked."

"I will search the room again."

"Are you looking for anything in particular?"

"Only things we have not yet previously found."

"Fine. Make a search cast."

The Warrior picks up his knuckle-bones, but pauses. "I am using all of Draag's inner resources of courage."

"Noted."

The knuckle-bones bounce across the table. "Nine successes!"

"You haven't found anything new."

"What about the food hatch?" asks the Jester.

"What about it?"

"Well I stayed in a place once where they had a sort of lift for food."

"A dumb waiter," says the Dealer.

"Well it was an orc place, so it wasn't noticeably dumber than their flesh-and-blood ones. But anyway, the kitchen would load the food into it, pull on a pulley to lift it upstairs, and then ring a bell thing. The food hatch on your cell might be one of those things."

A number of things displease the AllFather about this suggestion, starting – of course – with the fact that the Jester is even making it, given that his mortal is currently somewhere else entirely. Ever since the Warrior decided to create a whole new host of top leadership positions by slaughtering an entire shift crew he has been attempting to arrange a new set of possibilities by which the gods might complete their task.

He had Draag, Tallenna, Stone and Yann captured and imprisoned to keep them out of trouble while the raw anger of what they've done dissipates. He had Hill fall more than ten days worth of staircase for the same reason.

He is trying to create time for his players and the procedure they have to perform to enjoy it is rather simple.

They just have to shut up and sit still.

Behind the food hatch was a small space measuring around two and a half feet by two feet by eighteen inches, and it was undoubtedly a tribute to Draag's single mindedness that he'd managed to defy logic, reality and the fundamental laws of geometry by squeezing his armour-clad frame into it.

"Now remember," said a voice from somewhere that might have been his face, or his crotch, or both. "Shut the door, and then ask for mutton broth. We've had that before so they won't be suspicious."

Tallenna slid the door shut and then lowered her face to the small grill beside it. "Mutton broth!"

As always, there were no sounds from the hatch, just an unearthly silence for thirty seconds, followed by the chime that indicated that the meal was ready,

"Ready?" Yann asked her.

She nodded, and he slid the door open.

The smell of warm mutton broth wafted into the room.

"Do you need a little help getting out of there?" asked Tallenna.

"I suppose I now have to spend the next ten days sitting here covered with broth!" says the Warrior.

"You could ask the waiter for a jug of water," suggests the Jester, earning a black look from the Warrior.

"Fine! It is clear that we have no options save wait for this imbecile to finish climbing the staircase."

171

"I'll carry on climbing then, shall I?"

Ten days and 10,008 storeys later, Yrttttt announced that they had reached what he termed his "home level". This was news to Hill: every turn of the staircase bought them past a new but identical door, and whenever he poked his head out over the rail and looked upward he could see the shaft ascending towards an infinitely far vanishing point.

But Yrttttt's excitement to be home was clear.

"Level AB89, sector C83B!" he announced, holding the door open with a flourish.

"AB89, eh?" said Hill as he stepped through the door. "You know I've always wanted to come here but never thought I'd have the chance."

He paused in the doorway, and gazed out at what lay beyond.

When he was very young, his mother had soothed him to sleep by telling him the legends of the dwarfs. The tales of a short, stocky people who dwelt underground, spending their days crafting items of magnificence and their evenings drinking ale and breaking heads, had made a strong and lasting impression on the young halfling. In his boyhood dreams he'd walked the streets of huge and glittering underground cities; in his adulthood dreams he'd looted them.

The doorway led onto a long metal corridor lined with plain metal doors.

"Lead on Yrttttt my son," said a disappointed Hill.

"I shall take you to my spiritual mentor, Grzzztttt," said the lizard. "He shall know what to do!"

Grzzztttt turned out to be old and a little confused, with sagging scales and a memory span that hovered somewhere between "two year old toddler" and "goldfish".

"You say you are from... the outside?" he asked for the third, or perhaps the fourth, time. Like Yrttttt, he had a translation device around his neck. It didn't seem to be helping though.

"Yes," said Hill, patiently.

"What is the outside?"

"It is beyond here."

"Beyond Level AB89, sector C83B?"

"Beyond all the levels and all the sectors."

"I see." The lizard nodded, and looked at Yrttttt. "He must be from over by the Z sectors. They're pretty weird over there."

Hill sighed, and started over. "No, no. I'm from the outside."

The Jester points at the knuckle-bones in front of him. "Nine successes! If he still can't understand what I'm saying then he's an

172

to persuade Yrttttt to give me his translation device. Two, they might then notice that my lips aren't actually moving in time with what I'm saying. And three, and to be honest, I think this is the deal breaker, they might notice that I'm pink and fleshy like you and not green and scaly like them, and on that basis smell a rat – or whatever the lizard equivalent is."

"Some kind of small amphibian?" suggests the Sleeper.

"Yes, thank you. Anyway that's three good reasons for not trying that. If you give me a moment I can probably come up with a lot more, but I figure those are enough to be getting on with."

"Look! I was only trying to make a suggestion!"

"There must be a way out of this," says the Lady, casting a questioning glance at the AllFather, who merely nods. "We've just got to figure out what it is."

The Jester looks straight at the AllFather. "So there is a solution?"

"Well of course there is."

"Can you give us a clue?"

"No!" the AllFather protests. "How many times do we have to go through this? Challenge and satisfaction evaporate if I just drip feed you answers."

"Perhaps, but when they take their friends boredom and frustration with them I'd say it's a fair swap."

The AllFather gives him a very stern look. "Well I'm not in the business of giving clues."

"You always say that, but you usually cave in the end."

It is an accusation the AllFather finds no less annoying for being in the main true.

"Well I'm not caving now!" he snaps.

An image appears in his mind of Mr Six Days, wine glass in hand, surrounded by a retinue of early model nature spirit gods hanging onto his every word.

"You just need to think!"

"About what?"

"About how to get the information you need!"

If past conferences are any guide, Mr Six Days will no doubt talk of the "majestic sweep of history" and the "parabolic curve of progress". He will talk of telescopes that see the light of early creation, and of atom smashers, and of space probes splashing down into methane seas.

"Information you say?"

The AllFather is a little hazy on parabolas, has never felt the need for his creation to be constructed of anything more sophisticated than dust, and thinks that methane seas are the most ridiculous thing he's ever heard of. None of that will matter if he just has his own tale to tell."

"Yes! Information! It's what you need to plan things!"

"We need to plan?"

"Well, yes. I should have thought that was obvious."

The Jester casts his gaze across his fellow gods. "Okay, so there's some piece of information that will tell us how to get you guys out of there, and some kind of research we can do that will get it."

"Where do you go or what do you use to research?" asks the Lady.

"Libraries, museums, experts," says the Dealer.

The Warrior snaps his fingers together. "That net thing!"

"That will be it!" says the Jester, rubbing his hands together. He looks at the AllFather and gives him a smile of thanks that isn't entirely appreciated.

Hill prided himself on being a persuasive fellow, and persuading Yrttttt to put his study of lizard biology to one side required a good deal of persuasion. But once done, the lizard proved to be skilled in the ways of ferreting out information from the OverNet.

Hill avoided asking why.

It took some hours, and some of the archives they dug into were so old that Yrttttt needed his translation device to understand them.

"That's why I got it," he told Hill when Hill asked. "The old films are the best, but I like to follow the plot and stuff before they, you know?"

Hill really didn't want to know.

But eventually, in a note attached to a page in an archive of an archive, they found what they were looking for.

"That's actually pretty obvious," said Hill.

"How is it obvious?" asks the AllFather.

"Well the whole thing with the door was obvious misdirection, wasn't it?"

"In what way?" asks the Lady.

"Well in that by putting in something that looks like a door, he made us think that it actually was a door!"

"Well it could actually have been an actual door," says the AllFather.

"Yeah." The Jester snorts. "Right."

For eleven days the magic hole in the wall had fed them, producing on demand the food they asked for. Tasty food. Nutritious food. Food that filled the belly and soothed the mind.

But deep in his soul Yann knew that it wasn't food. The bread that he now ate had not been milled from wheat given life by the gods of fertility and ripened by the gods of the sun. No beast had been sacrificed to make the soup he now slurped, nor vegetables grown and dug.

It wasn't real.

Nothing was real in this horrid realm of synthetic sunlight and metal floor. And yet, this was reality. This was real. It was the realm outside that was fake.

178

under-butler's accidental kicking of his tricycle's rear wheel. It had felt good. He still warmly remembered the contentment he'd felt as he peddled down the corridor and away from the expanding pool of blood.

He liked killing.

Especially when he was bored.

And right now he was very, very bored.

He stood up and pulled DeathSinger from its scabbard. "I'm going to go out and look for rioters. Anyone want to come with me?"

The argument has been going for some while now now and is showing signs of turning nasty. The AllFather puts on his most placating voice and posture. "No, no, I'm not trying to tell you what you can do. I'm just pointing out that whatever you do, it really is for the best if you all do it together."

The Warrior shrugs. "Fine. As I said. They can come with me if they wish."

The Lady interjects. "Well we might be more likely to do that if you had some plan beyond mere random violence."

"Yeah," says the Jester. "If you were, say, planning on assaulting and capturing the Central Pumping Plant and dumping nutrients in yourself, that would be a plan we could consider. We'd turn it down, of course, what with it being not much more than a psychotic suicide note written by a depressed lemming with a death-wish–"

Draag raised his sword high. "Comrades! I am going to capture the Central Pumping Plant and restore the nutrient flow. Who is with me?"

"That was actually just an exam–"

Yann stood, and crossed the room to stand beside Draag. "I'll fight alongside you."

"I'm sorry?" splutters the Jester.

The Dealer pauses for a moment, and then speaks. "I said I'll fight with him."

"But it's a suicidal plan! Even if we capture the place, how long are we supposed to hold it for? Do we even have a plan for afterwards?"

"Yann cares not for such things. Life has no meaning for him now. Creation itself has no meaning for him now. He has no future save sacrifice or death."

The Lady breaks in. "You're still sulking then?"

"That's a completely unfair accusation to make Mistress Lady, and one, if I may be so bold, that is beneath you."

She raises an eyebrow, but says nothing.

The AllFather clears his throat. "I know I'm supposed to be merely an impartial arbiter of fate, but I should perhaps stress that there are many avenues available to you, and that you really should spend some time considering all your options."

"We have thought," says the Warrior. "And we have considered. Now we are acting. Who is with us?"

Stone looked up from the stool upon which he sat.

"Are we going somewhere then? Sorry. Didn't realise."

He got up and walked to stand beside Yann. "I'll follow him," he said, pointing at the barbarian.

The Jester throws up his hands in horror. "Oh what the hell, it'll probably be a laugh."

Tallenna's heart thumped hard in her chest like a hammer upon her soul. Her four companions stood both opposite her, and in opposition to her. Logic and intuition both told her that the course of action they intended to pursue was terribly, terribly wrong. But deep-taught duty told her that if this was the path they did indeed take, then it was one that she, their comrade, must walk with them.

She turned to Hill, who had been the last of her allies.

"But you said this was a suicide mission?"

"Yeah, well it is. But it probably won't end up that way."

"What do you mean?"

"Whatever happens, something will happen to make it turn out alright in the end. Something always does, doesn't it? Time after time we've been so far down shit creek we're damn near out in the ocean, and every single time we've managed to pull something together and get out in one piece."

Tallenna had lived her life in the pursuit of logic and reason. She didn't want to hear this, but the halfling wasn't stopping.

"Maybe it's fate. Maybe someone up there likes us. Maybe me and the gods have got the same bookie and he's pulling strings up there 'til I get my account straight. Whatever. It always seems to work out okay whatever we do, and however badly we screw up, and I figure that ain't likely to change just yet."

His words struck doubts within her she hadn't known she had. Was this what Yann had felt when he saw the control room? She didn't know what she feared most. The fact that Hill might be wrong.

Or the fact that he might be right.

Best Friends

A Role-Playing Game About Girlfriends
And All Their Petty Hatreds

"**Best Friends** gets my award for most **awesome** and **elegant** currency mechanic."

—Paul Czege
author of *My Life with Master*

A **role-playing game** for **four or more friends**.
Written and illustrated by Gregor Hutton.

Box Ninja

Available from IndiePressRevolution.com

http://boxninja.com

Breinigsville, PA USA
12 December 2009
229122BV00001B/95/P

Unseemly Haste

Book 4 of the Concordia Wells Mysteries

K.B. OWEN

Author of *Dangerous and Unseemly, Unseemly Pursuits &*
Unseemly Ambition

Unseemly Haste

Book 4 of the Concordia Wells Mysteries

Copyright © 2015 Kathleen Belin Owen

Printed in the United States of America

Cover design by Melinda VanLone, BookCoverCorner.com

Formatting by Debora Lewis
arenapublishing.org

ISBN-13: 978-0-9912368-6-2

For my sons,

Patrick, Liam, and Corey.

May your own journeys be happy

and full of adventure.